"You're Flirting With Me? Why?"

Caleb debated for a moment before answering. But then he reminded himself he was in Colorado. People were forthright around here. And he owed Mandy no less than she was giving him.

"Because you're real," he told her. "When you laugh, it's because you're happy. When you argue, it's because you have a point to make. And when your eyes smolder, it's because you're interested in me."

"I'm not interested in you."

"But you are." He smoothed a stray lock of her hair and tucked it behind one ear. "That's what's so amazing about you. Your body language doesn't lie."

"And if my body language slaps you across the face?"

"I hope it'll be because I've done something to deserve it." Because then the slap would be worth it.

* * *

To find out more about Desire's
upcoming books and to chat with authors and editors,
become a fan of Harlequin Desire on Facebook
www.facebook.com/HarlequinDesire or follow us
on Twitter www.twitter.com/desireeditors!

Dear Reader,

Welcome to the first book of the Colorado Cattle Barons series from Harlequin Desire. I have a deep fondness for cowboy heroes, and this series will allow me to indulge myself by writing a whole string of them.

In book one, millionaire Caleb Terrell returns to his family's Colorado ranch, following the death of his abusive father. There, he meets sexy, down-to-earth neighbor Mandy Jacobs, the key to finding Caleb's missing twin brother, Reed. While Mandy opens the door to painful childhood memories, she also shows Caleb the pathway to love and forgiveness.

I sincerely hope you enjoy *A Cowboy Comes Home*. And I hope you'll look for Caleb's brother, Reed, along with Mandy's siblings, in future Colorado Cattle Barons books. I'd love to hear from you, so please feel free to drop me a line through my website, barbaradunlop.com.

Barbara Dunlop

BARBARA DUNLOP

A COWBOY COMES HOME

Harlequin®

Desire

Recycling programs
for this product may
not exist in your area.

ISBN-13: 978-0-373-73147-3

A COWBOY COMES HOME

www.Harlequin.com

Printed in U.S.A.

Books by Barbara Dunlop

Harlequin Desire

An After-Hours Affair #2108
†*A Cowboy Comes Home* #2134

Silhouette Desire

Thunderbolt over Texas #1704
Marriage Terms #1741
The Billionaire's Bidding #1793
The Billionaire Who Bought Christmas #1836
Beauty and the Billionaire #1853
Marriage, Manhattan Style #1897
Transformed Into the Frenchman's Mistress #1929
*Seduction and the CEO #1996
*In Bed with the Wrangler #2003
*His Convenient Virgin Bride #2009
The CEO's Accidental Bride #2062
Billionaire Baby Dilemma #2073

*Montana Millionaires: The Ryders
†Colorado Cattle Barons

Other titles by this author available in ebook.

BARBARA DUNLOP

writes romantic stories while curled up in a log cabin in Canada's far north, where bears outnumber people and it snows six months of the year. Fortunately she has a brawny husband and two teenage children to haul firewood and clear the driveway while she sips cocoa and muses about her upcoming chapters. Barbara loves to hear from readers. You can contact her through her website, www.barbaradunlop.com.

For Carla Daum and Jane Porter
One-Hundred Books Later

* * *

Don't miss February's A COWBOY IN MANHATTAN,
the next book in this series by
USA TODAY bestselling author
Barbara Dunlop!

COLORADO CATTLE BARONS:
From the mountains to the boardroom, these men
have everything under control—except their hearts.

One

Dust plumes scattered beneath Caleb Terrell's loafers as he approached the front steps of his former home, looking for the brother who'd despised him for ten long years. A copy of his late father's will was snapped into his Bulgari briefcase, and a million, disturbing questions swirled inside his brain. The Terrell Cattle Company hadn't changed much. The two-story brick house had been meticulously maintained, while the crisp, northern-Colorado mountain air still held the familiar tang of wheatgrass and ponderosa pine.

The soles of his shoes met the smooth wood of the wide, front porch, and for a fleeting moment he wished he'd stopped in Lyndon and changed into blue jeans and boots. But he banished the impulse. He was a businessman now, not a cowboy. And the last thing he wanted to do was feel at home.

His brother, Reed, wouldn't be remotely happy to see him, but outrageous times called for outrageous measures. Reed would have to deal with it.

Caleb briefly toyed with the idea of bursting in unannounced. He owned the place, after all, and Reed had been dodging his calls for over a week. To be fair, Caleb hadn't tried to contact his fraternal twin brother in ten years. Then again, in all that time, Reed hadn't tried to contact Caleb, either.

But now, their father was dead. Caleb wouldn't have set foot on the Terrell ranch in any other circumstance. He'd probably have been shot if he'd tried. Which made the contents of the will that much more baffling.

He gave three short, sharp knocks.

In the moments of silence that followed, he glanced around the ranch yard, refreshing his memory and bracing himself for the conversation to come.

The main barn had been recently painted a dark green. The square horse corrals were still meticulously maintained, their straight rails gleaming white in the afternoon sunshine. He knew every angle was precisely ninety degrees, and the posts were exactly six feet apart, rail centers at twenty-four-inch intervals.

Beyond the yard, black angus cattle dotted the summer green, hillside meadows between groves of aspen and pine. And the snowy peaks of the Rockies rose up to the misty sky. Caleb blinked against the blinding sun, refocusing closer in.

Half a dozen pickup trucks were backed up in formation in front of the equipment sheds. A freshly washed combine, cultivator and hay truck sat on the far side of the barn, and a few dozen chickens were pecking the ground around the tires. In one of the pens, a black horse whinnied and bucked, tossing its glossy mane as it ran the length of the enclosure before stopping short at the fence, nostrils flaring in annoyance.

Caleb didn't recognize the animal. No surprise there. Though there had been a time when he'd been able to name every one of the fifty plus horses at Terrell. He inhaled once more, this time catching the sharp scent of manure. His spine stiffened with a latent memory of his father's quick temper. Yeah, most things had stayed the same around here, and he didn't care to revisit any of them.

As soon as he straightened out the mess with the inheritance, he'd climb back into his rented Escalade, head for the Lyndon airport and take the Active Equipment jet back to his corporate headquarters in Chicago.

Sayonara Colorado.

He turned back to the door and knocked again.

This time, there was a sound on the other side. But it was a light, quick step crossing the living-room floor—so, not his brother, Reed.

The door swung full open, and Caleb came face-to-face with a beautiful, brunette woman. She was maybe five feet five, dressed in a cowl-necked, navy T-shirt with four buttons leaving an open V-neck. Her hair was long and glossy, her lips a dark coral pink, skin smooth, brows gently arched and her moss-green eyes clear and assessing.

She looked vaguely familiar. Or maybe that was just wishful thinking. Even in faded blue jeans and scuffed brown boots, she definitely looked like someone Caleb would like to know. His instantaneous attraction was quickly tempered by the thought that she might belong to his brother—a girlfriend, maybe even a wife.

His glance dipped reflexively to her left hand. No ring. But that didn't mean she wasn't Reed's.

"Are you selling…something?" she prompted, glancing from his silk tie to his briefcase. Her melodic, slightly husky voice sent a vibration through the center of Caleb's chest.

It took him a moment to respond. "I'm looking for Reed."

Her delicate brows sloped closer together with curiosity. "Is he expecting you?"

"I called a few days ago," Caleb offered evasively. He hadn't spoken to his brother, only left voice-mail messages, and he wasn't about to discuss his personal business with a stranger.

She crossed her arms over her chest and canted a slim, denim covered hip to one side. "Are you saying Reed invited you here?"

Caleb gave into curiosity. "Who are you?"

"Who are you?"

There it was again, that feeling that he'd met her somewhere before. "You live here?"

"None of your business."

"Where's Reed?"

She stilled for a split second, her soft, coral mouth pursing into a sexy moue. "Also, none of your business."

He struggled to be annoyed, but he found himself intrigued. "Are you going to tell me anything?"

She shook her head.

"Have we met before?" he asked.

"Is that a line?"

"It's a question."

"It's been my experience that most lines are delivered in the form of a question."

Caleb felt himself crack a reluctant smile, and her green eyes sparkled in return.

He watched her for a few moments, then conceded defeat, shifting his briefcase from his right hand before holding it out to her. "Caleb Terrell."

Her gorgeous eyes went wide and round. "Caleb?"

Before he could react, she squealed and threw herself into his arms. "You came home!"

His free arm automatically wrapped around her slender waist, returning the hug and holding her lithe body against his own. He inhaled the sweet scent of her hair and found himself desperately hoping she wasn't Reed's girlfriend.

She pulled back and gazed up into his eyes. "You don't remember me?"

He was forced to shake his head, admitting he did not.

She socked the front of his shoulder with the heel of her hand. "It's Mandy."

Caleb felt his jaw go lax. "Mandy Jacobs?"

She nodded, and he pulled her into another hug. Not that they'd been particularly close. She'd been thirteen to his seventeen when he'd left home. He was twenty-seven now. And it felt astonishingly good to hold her in his arms.

He let the hug go on a little too long, then reluctantly let her go.

"You missed the funeral." Her tone was half regretful, half accusing as she backed her way inside the house, gesturing for him to follow.

"I didn't come back for the funeral," he told her soberly as he took a step over the threshold. Reminded of his reason for being here, his mood swung back to determination.

"He was your father," she chided, turning to walk around the corner from the foyer and into the big living room.

Caleb followed, letting his silence speak for itself. Unless Mandy was hopelessly naive, she knew the history of the Terrell family. Wilton Terrell might have been Caleb's father, but he was also the meanest son of a bitch in northwestern Colorado.

Inside the startlingly familiar room, he glanced around, attempting to orient himself. Why was Mandy here, and where was Reed? "So, you and Reed are…"

She shook her head. "He's not here."

"I can see that." It was a big house, two stories, four bedrooms, but if Reed had been around, Mandy's squeal would have brought him running. Now, Caleb found himself impatient to qualify her role. "You live here?"

Her look went blank. "Huh?"

He enunciated his next words. "Do you live here?"

"Are you asking me if I'm sleeping with your brother?"

"I'm asking if you're in a relationship with him, yes." That was the most obvious answer for her presence.

"I'm not." Her left eye twitched. "Either of those things."

"Okay."

Good. Very good. Not that it mattered to Caleb. Nothing about Lyndon Valley or the Terrell ranch mattered to Caleb. This was a temporary glitch on the thoroughfare of his life. Mandy was irrelevant.

Her tone turned tart. "But how very polite of you to inquire about my sex life."

"You're here, and he's not," Caleb reasoned. She'd answered the front door, appeared very much at home. It wasn't such a stretch to think she lived here.

She traced a finger along the beveled edge of a polished cedar side table. "I came up here to check things out." Then a cloud of concern darkened her expression. "I got worried."

"Why were you worried?"

"Because nobody's seen Reed since the funeral five days ago."

Mandy Jacobs had been Reed's close friend for nearly ten years. Before that, she'd felt something close to hero worship for him in high school, ever since the day he'd rescued her when her bikini top flew off as she dove into the Stump Lake swimming hole. The boys in her own grade had howled with laughter, stopping her girlfriends from coming into the water to help her, waiting with wide-eyed anticipation for the numbing cold to force her from the lake.

Just as she was about to give in and cover her dignity as best she could manage, Reed had come along and read the younger boys the riot act. He'd stripped off his boots and waded up to his waist, handing her his own T-shirt. He'd never even peeked while, teeth chattering and toes tingling, she'd struggled her way into the shirt while under water. And then he'd threatened the younger boys with dire consequences if they dared to tease her about it in the future.

When she came home after two years in college in Denver, she and Reed had grown closer still. Over the years, she'd learned about his mother's death, his father's cruelty and the reasons behind his fraternal twin brother, Caleb, leaving the valley.

Reed had no siblings left at home, and Mandy's two brothers did nothing but tease her. Her oldest sister, Abigail, had been a bookworm, while her younger sister, Katrina, had gone away to boarding school when she was only ten. If Mandy could have chosen a brother, it would have been Reed.

This morning, genuinely worried and determined to track him down, she'd let herself into the familiar house, listened to his phone messages, hunted her way through his letter mail, even checked his closet before realizing she wouldn't know if some of his clothes were missing or not. She did know his wallet was gone. His watch wasn't lying around and his favorite Stetson wasn't hanging on the peg in the front entry hall.

She had to believe he had left the ranch willingly. The man was built like a mountain. She couldn't imagine anyone forcing him to do anything he didn't want to do.

Still, she was very glad Caleb had shown up when he did. Something definitely wasn't right, and she could use his help to figure out what had happened.

Caleb clunked his briefcase down on the hardwood floor, interrupting her musings as he straightened beside the brown leather couch that sat in front of the picture window.

His gaze pierced hers. "Define *missing?*"

"Reed left the cemetery after the funeral," Mandy explained, casting her memory back again to the events of last week, hunting for little details she might have missed that would give her a clue to what happened. "He drove off in one of the ranch pickup trucks. I assumed he was coming back here."

She focused on the row of pictures along the fireplace mantel, zeroing in on a recent one of Reed at the Lyndon Rodeo. "We all came over to the house afterward for refreshments. I didn't see him, but I didn't think that was particularly odd. He'd just lost his father and, you know, he might have wanted to be alone."

From behind her, Caleb's voice was cool. "Are you trying to tell me Reed was mourning our father?"

She turned back to face him while she framed her answer. She couldn't help contrasting the two brothers. They were about as different as two men could get. They'd both been attractive teenagers who'd grown into very handsome men. But where Reed was rugged and rangy, Caleb was much more urbane and refined.

Reed was nearly six-four, deep-chested, bulky in his arms and legs, and about as strong as an ox. His hair was dark, his eyes darker. While Caleb was closer to six-one, broad shouldered, but with leaner muscles, a chiseled chin and bright blue, intelligent, observant eyes. His hair was a lighter brown, his voice bass instead of baritone.

"Mandy?" Caleb prompted, and there was something about the sound of her name on his lips that made her heart thud an extra beat. Where on earth had that come from?

"I doubt he was mourning your father," she acknowledged.

If anything, Reed and Wilton's relationship had deteriorated after Caleb left. Wilton wasn't capable of anything but criticism, no matter how hard Reed worked. And no matter how much Reed accomplished on the ranch, his father wasn't satisfied and told him so on a regular basis.

Intimidated by the man, Mandy had visited the Terrell house only when Wilton was away. Thankfully, he was away quite often. The very definition of a crotchety old man, he seemed to prefer the company of cattle to humans, and he spent many nights in line shacks on the range.

She'd done everything she could to support Reed. When she was sixteen and Reed was twenty, Wilton had ended a particularly hostile argument by whacking Reed's shoulder with a two-by-four. Mandy had impulsively offered to marry Reed so he could move to the neighboring Jacobs ranch.

But he'd had laughed at her and tousled her hair, telling her he loved her like a sister, not a wife, and he wouldn't turn his back on his father ever again. And by then, he was big enough to defend himself against Wilton.

"He should have left when I did," Caleb broke into her thoughts again, his voice brittle.

"*You* should have stayed," Mandy countered, giving him her unvarnished opinion. If Caleb had been around, it would have been two against one, and Wilton would not have gotten away with so much cruelty.

Caleb's eyes crackled like agates. "And rewarded him for

killing my mother, by breaking my back for him day after day?"

"Reed saw it differently." Mandy understood just how differently Reed had viewed the situation. And she admired him for it.

The Terrell Cattle Company had been the merging of both Wilton Terrell's family holdings and those of his young wife, Sasha's. After her death, through thick and thin, Reed had vowed to protect his mother's heritage. He had plans for the ranch, for his future, ways to honor his mother's memory.

Which made his disappearance, particularly now, even more confusing. Where *was* he?

"Reed was a fool," said Caleb.

Mandy found herself taking a step forward, squaring her shoulders, hands curling into fists by her sides, her anger rising in her friend's defense. "I love Reed."

"I thought you said—"

"Like a *brother*."

"Yeah?" Caleb scoffed, blue eyes glaring right back at her. "Why don't you tell me what that's like?"

His mocking tone was at odds with the trace of hurt that flashed through his eyes, and her anger immediately dissipated.

"Why did you come?" she found herself asking.

Did she dare hope Caleb had reconciliation on his mind? She'd be thrilled to see the two brothers bury the hatchet. She knew that, deep down, Reed missed his brother, and she had to believe Caleb missed Reed.

Suddenly, she remembered one of the letters she'd sorted this morning. Her heart lifted, and her chest hummed with excitement. That had to be the answer. "He *was* expecting you."

"What?"

She pivoted on her heel and headed for the kitchen, beelining to the pile of correspondence that hadn't yielded a single clue to Reed's whereabouts.

Caleb's footfalls sounded in the hallway behind her as she

entered the bright, butter-yellow kitchen, with its gleaming redwood cabinets and granite countertops.

"Here it is." She extracted a white envelope with Caleb's name scrawled across the front. It hadn't made sense to her at the time, but Reed must have known his brother would be here. Maybe this was the clue she needed.

She strode back across the big, bright kitchen and handed the envelope to Caleb. "Open it," she demanded impatiently.

Caleb frowned. "I didn't tell him I was coming." The messages had been a cryptic "call me, we need to talk." He hadn't doubted for a second Reed would understand.

"Then why did he leave you a letter? It was sitting on the island when I got here this morning." She pointed out the spot with her finger.

Caleb heaved a deep breath, hooking his thumb beneath the end of the flap and tearing open the flimsy paper.

He extracted a single, folded sheet and dropped the envelope onto the countertop next to the telephone. He unfolded the paper, staring at it for a brief moment.

Then he uttered a sharp, foul cussword.

Mandy startled, not at the word, but at the tone. Unable to control her curiosity, she looked around the paper, her head next to Caleb's shoulder and read Reed's large, bold handwriting. The message said: *Choke on it.*

She blinked and glanced up at Caleb. "I don't understand. What does it mean?"

"It means my brother's temper hasn't changed one bit in the past ten years."

"Do you know where he went?" The cryptic message didn't help Mandy, but maybe Caleb understood.

Caleb growled at the paper. "You stupid, stupid idiot."

"What?" Mandy demanded.

He crumpled the paper into a tight ball, emitting a cold laugh. "He doesn't trust me. He actually thinks I'd screw my own brother."

"Screw him how?" She'd been telling herself Reed was off

on his own somewhere, reconciling what had to be conflicting emotions about losing such a difficult father. But now Caleb had her worried.

He stared down at her, blue eyes rock-hard, jaw set in an implacable line. She could almost see the debate going on inside his head.

Finally, he made a decision and spoke. "Wilton Terrell, in his infinite wisdom, has left his entire estate, including the Terrell Cattle Company, to his son...Caleb."

Mandy braced herself on the edge of the island, her breath hitching inside her chest. "He left it to *you?*"

"He left it to me."

A thousand emotions burst through her. This was colossally unfair. It was ridiculously and maliciously, reprehensibly... Reed had given his blood, sweat and tears to this place, and now Caleb was simply going to ride in and take over?

Her voice was breathless with disgust. "How could you?"

"How could *I—*" He gave a snort of derision. "Wilton did it."

"But you're the one who benefited."

"I'm here to give it *back,* Mandy. But thank you for the faith in my character. Your low opinion of me is matched only by my idiot brother's."

"You're going to give it back?" She couldn't keep the skepticism from her tone. Caleb was simply going to walk away from a ranch worth tens of millions of dollars?

"I live in Chicago now. Why in the hell would I want to come back to a place I hated, that holds nothing but bitter memories? And he's my brother. We hate each other, but we don't *hate* each other."

Judging by his affronted expression and the passion in his tone, Caleb truly was going to do the honorable thing. But Reed must have been as skeptical as Mandy. The anger in the note was plain as day, and he'd obviously hightailed it out of there before he had to watch his brother come in and take over.

Fresh worry percolated to life inside her. "We have to find him. We have to explain and bring him home."

"He's not a lost puppy."

"He's your brother."

Caleb seemed singularly unmoved. "What exactly does that mean?"

His brother's house was the last place Caleb wanted to be. He didn't want to eat in this kitchen or sit in that living room, and he definitely had no desire to go upstairs and sleep in his old bedroom.

He'd had enough déjà vu already.

The kitchen might as well have been frozen in time. A spider plant sat in the middle of the island, serving utensils upside down in a white container next to the stove, a bulletin board above the phone, a fruit bowl under the light switch and the coffeemaker beneath the built-in microwave.

He knew the sugar would be on the third shelf of the pantry, the milk in the door of the stainless-steel refrigerator and the coffee beans on the second shelf in the pantry next to the dining room. He'd kill for a cup of coffee, but there was no way he was making himself at home.

Mandy, on the other hand, seemed to feel completely at home. She'd perched herself on one of the high, black-cushioned chairs at the center island, one booted foot propped on the cross piece, one swinging in a small arc as she dialed her phone.

"Are you here often?" He couldn't help asking. He didn't remember anyone ever looking relaxed in this house.

She raised her phone to her ear and gave a small, wry smile. "Only when your father was away. Reed and I used to drink cheap wine and play poker."

"Just the two of you?" Caleb arched a brow. He didn't yet have a handle on the relationship between his brother and Mandy.

She raked her loose hair back from her forehead. "I told you

I wasn't sleeping with him." She left a deliberate pause. "When I stayed over, I slept in your bed. Oh, hey, Seth," she said into the phone.

Absurdly rattled by her taunt, Caleb withdrew into the living room to clear his head. This trip was not going even remotely as he'd planned.

It was two hours to the Lyndon airport. He could drive there and fly back to Chicago tonight. Or he could get a hotel room in Lyndon. Or he could stay here and figure out what on earth to do next.

His gaze strayed to the staircase at the opposite end of the living room. His old bedroom was up there. Where, apparently, Mandy had been sleeping. Of course, she could have been lying about that, simply amusing herself by messing with his head.

Then again, even if she had slept in his bed, why should he care? He didn't. The woman could sleep wherever she wanted.

Her footfalls sounded on the kitchen tiles. Seconds later, she strode through the archway between the kitchen and the living room, tucking her phone into the front pocket of her jeans. "Seth's going to send a couple of hands."

"Send them where?"

She did a double take. "Here, of course."

"Why?"

"To help you out."

"I didn't ask for help." Caleb didn't mean to sound ungrateful, but he didn't need Mandy waltzing in and making decisions for him. He didn't know what happened next, but he knew he'd be the guy calling the shots.

She blinked. "I know. I did it as a favor."

"Next time, please ask permission."

"You want me to ask for permission to do a favor?"

"I want you to ask permission to meddle in my business."

"Meddling? You call lending you two highly qualified hands to take care of your ranch while we look for your brother *meddling*?"

Caleb took in the determined tilt of her chin, the squared

shoulders that said she was ready for a scrap and the animated flash in her jewel-bright eyes. He decided it wasn't the right time for a fight.

"Next time," he told her more softly, "please ask first."

"I wouldn't worry about there being a next time."

Fine. No problem. He'd dealt with everything else in his life without help.

He'd find his brother. He'd find him fast and get his life back to normal.

He couldn't help thinking about how his financial lawyer, Danielle Marin, was going to react to him being stuck in Colorado.

Active Equipment was at a critical point in setting up a new division in South America. Danielle was wading her way through Brazil's complicated banking and accounting regulations.

Mandy moved in closer. "What are you going to do now?"

"Find Reed." And drag him home.

"And in the meantime? The ranch? The animals?"

"I'll deal with it."

A mocking lilt came into Mandy's voice. "Sure would be nice if you had a little help."

"Sure would be nice if you minded your own business."

"I'm only doing my duty as a neighbor."

"Are you going for the good-neighbor merit badge?"

She perked up. "There's a badge?"

"Were you always this much of a smart-ass?"

"You don't remember what I was like?"

"You were four grades behind me. I barely noticed you."

"I thought you were hot."

Caleb went still.

"Schoolgirl fantasy," Mandy finished smoothly. "I didn't know your true character back then."

"You don't know my true character now," he retorted.

But her words triggered some kind of hormonal reaction deep inside him. *He* thought *she* was hot, right here, right now, right this very minute. And that was a complication this situation definitely didn't need.

"You married?" he asked her hopefully. "Engaged?"

She wiggled her bare left hand in front of his face.

"Seeing someone?" he pressed, praying for the yes that would make him honor bound to quit thinking of her naked in his arms.

"Why do you want to know?"

"I wondered who I should pity."

Despite the insult, their gazes locked. They flared, and then smoldered. He couldn't seem to tamp down his unspoken desire.

"No," she told him flatly.

"I didn't ask you anything." He didn't want to kiss her. He *wouldn't* want to kiss her.

She tipped her head to a challenging angle, her rich, dark hair flowing like a curtain. "I'm helping you find your brother. Don't get any ideas."

"I didn't ask for your help." What he really wanted was for her to go away and stay away so he could keep him emotions on an even keel.

"You're getting it, anyway, neighbor."

"There isn't actually a badge, you know."

"I want him back, too."

It wasn't that Caleb had an interest in ferrying Reed back to Lyndon Valley. He had an interest in the Terrell ranch no longer being his problem. And there was more than one way to accomplish that.

"I could sell the place," he pointed out.

She stiffened, drawing back in obvious astonishment. "You wouldn't."

"I could."

"I won't let you."

The threat was laughable. "How're you going to stop me?"

She lifted her chin. "I'll appeal to your honor and principles."

"Fresh out," he told her honestly, his desire for her starting a slow burn in his body. There was certainly no honor in lusting after his brother's neighbor.

She shook her head in denial, the tip of her tongue touching her bottom lip. "You're here, aren't you? You came all the way out here to give the ranch back to Reed. You can't undo all those good intentions because you've been slowed down by a day or so."

Caleb hesitated. The faster the better as far as he was concerned. "You think we can find him in a day or so?"

"Sure," she said with breezy conviction. "How hard can it be?"

Caleb wasn't touching that one.

But the flash in her eyes told him she'd heard the double-entendre as clearly as he did. She held up a warning finger. "I told you not to get any ideas."

"You have a vivid imagination."

"And you have a transparent expression. Don't ever play poker."

"Well, not with you."

"So, you admit I'm right?" Her expression held a hint of triumph.

"I can control myself if you can."

"There's nothing for me to control."

"You think I'm hot," he reminded her.

"When I was thirteen and underage."

"You're not underage now."

She pointed to him and then back to herself. "You and me, Caleb."

Sensual anticipation shot through his chest.

But she wasn't finished speaking. "Are going to find your brother, give him back his ranch and then go our respective ways."

Caleb squelched his ridiculous disappointment. What had he expected her to say?

Two

Having escaped to the Terrell's front porch and perched herself on the railing, Mandy tried not to think about the sensual awareness that flared inside her every time Caleb spoke.

And when he'd hugged her.

Hoo boy. She fanned herself with her white Stetson, remembering the tingling sensation that flowed across her skin and the glow that had warmed the pit of her stomach as he'd pressed his body against hers. Though the brothers were twins, she'd never felt anything remotely like that in a hug from Reed.

She heard the sound she'd been waiting for and saw a Jacobs ranch pickup truck careen up the driveway. She stuffed the hat back on her head as the truck caught air on the last pothole before spraying gravel while it spun in the turnaround and rocked to a halt. Two Jacobs ranch hands exited the passenger side, giving her a wave as they headed for the barn, while her brother Travis emerged from the driver's, anchoring his worn hat on his head and striding toward her.

"And?" Travis demanded as he approached, brows going up.

Mandy jabbed her thumb toward the front doorway just as Caleb filled the frame.

At six-two, with long legs, all lanky muscle, Travis easily took the stairs two at a time.

"Came to see for myself," he told Caleb, looking him up and down before offering his hand.

Caleb stepped outside and shook it, while Mandy slid off the rail, her boot heels clunking down on the porch.

"Good to see you, Travis," Caleb offered in a steady voice.

"Figured Seth had to be lying," said Travis, shoulders square, gaze assessing. "But here you are. A little uptight and overgroomed, but at least you didn't go soft on us."

"You were expecting a pot belly and a double chin?"

"And a pasty-white complexion."

"Sorry to disappoint you."

Travis shrugged. "What brought you back?"

Caleb's gaze slid to Mandy.

Travis glanced between them. "What?"

Caleb hesitated, obviously debating whether or not to reveal the information about the will.

"Travis can keep a secret," Mandy offered, moving toward them. Her family would be in a better position to help Caleb if he'd be honest with them.

Travis tipped his chin to a challenging angle, confronting Caleb. "What did you do?"

"Nothing," Caleb stated levelly. "I'm solving a problem, not creating one. But I remember gossip spreading like wildfire around here."

"Welcome home," Mandy put in, struggling to keep the sarcasm from her voice.

Caleb frowned at her. There was nothing salacious in his expression, no inappropriate message in his eyes. Still, the mere fact that he was looking at her sent a flush across her skin.

"Come back to dance on your daddy's grave?" Travis asked Caleb.

"You want a beer?" Caleb offered. Surprisingly, there was no annoyance in his tone at Travis's crass remark.

Mandy took the opportunity to escape from Caleb's proximity again, passing through the doorway and calling over her shoulder. "I'll get them."

She headed straight down the hall to the kitchen at the back of the house, shaking off the buzz of arousal. There was no denying the chemical attraction between her and Caleb, but that didn't mean she had to give in to it. Sure, he was a great-looking guy. He had an undeniably sexy voice, and he could pull of a Saville Row suit.

She had no doubt he'd look equally good in blue jeans and a Western-cut shirt. When they'd hugged, she'd felt his chest, stomach, thighs and arms, so she knew he was rock-solid with muscle. Whatever he'd been doing in Chicago for the past ten years, it wasn't sitting behind a desk.

She checked the wayward track of her brain and extracted three bottles of beer from the refrigerator, heading back down the hall.

When she arrived on the porch, Caleb had obviously brought Travis up to speed on the will. The two men had made themselves comfortable in the painted, wood-slat chairs. Mandy handed out the beers, her fingertips grazing Caleb's as he accepted his. She refused to look in his eyes, but the touch sent an electrical current coursing the length of her arm.

She backed away and perched herself on the wide railing, one leg canted across the rail, the other dangling between the slats.

"Just when you think a guy can't get any nastier," said Travis, twisting off the cap of his beer bottle.

Caleb took a swig of his own beer. "Only Wilton could screw up our lives from the grave."

Mandy had to agree with that. It looked as if Caleb's father had deliberately driven a new wedge between his two sons. The only way to repair the damage was to tell Reed about Caleb's offer to return the ranch.

"How are we going to find him?" she asked.

"We won't," said Travis, "if he doesn't want to be found."

"Probably doesn't," said Caleb. "Which means he's finally come to his senses and left this place in his dust."

"He thinks you're stealing his ranch," Mandy corrected, her voice rising on the accusation.

"Then why didn't he call me and talk about it? I'm listed."

"He probably thought you'd gloat," she guessed.

"Your faith in me is inspiring."

She hadn't meant it as an insult. "I was speculating on what Reed might think. I wasn't saying what I personally thought." She took a swig of the cold, bitter brew. It wasn't her favorite beverage, but sometimes it was the only thing going, so she'd learned to adapt.

"You thought I was going to keep the ranch," Caleb reminded her.

"But I believed you when you said you wouldn't," she countered.

"You want points for that?"

"Or a merit badge." The joke was out before she could stop it.

Caleb gave a half smile. Then he seemed to contemplate her for a long, drawn out moment. "I should just sell the damn thing."

"Well, that would be quite the windfall, wouldn't it?"

"You think I'd keep the money?"

She stilled, taking in his affronted expression. Oops. She swallowed. "Well..."

Caleb shook his head in obvious disgust, his tone flat. "I'd give the money to Reed, Mandy."

"Reed wants the ranch, not the money," she pointed out, attempting to cover the blunder.

"Then why isn't he here fighting for it?"

"Excellent question," Travis jumped in. "If it was me, I'd fight you tooth and nail. Hell, I'd lie, cheat and steal to get my land back."

"So, where is he?" Caleb's question was directed at Mandy. "I'm going to find out," she vowed.

Two days later, Mandy was no closer to an answer. Caleb, on the other hand, was moving his alternative plan along at lighting speed, having decided it was most efficient for him to stay on the ranch for now. He had a real-estate broker on retainer, an appraiser marching around the Terrell ranch and a photographer compiling digital shots for the broker's website. He'd told her that if they didn't find Reed in the next few days, the ranch was going on the market.

Trying to keep her activities logical and rational, despite the ticking clock, Mandy had gone from checking Reed's web-browser history for hotel sites, to trying his cell phone one more time, to calling the hospitals within a three-hundred-mile radius, just in case.

At noon, tired, frustrated and hungry, she wandered into the Terrell kitchen. She found a chicken breast in the freezer, cheese in the refrigerator along with half a jar of salsa, and some tomatoes, peppers and onions in the crisper.

Assuming Caleb and the appraiser would be hungry when they finished their work, she put the chicken breast in the microwave and set it to defrost. She found a thick skillet, flour, shortening and a rolling pin, and started mixing up a batch of homemade tortilla shells.

When Caleb walked in half an hour later, she was chopping her way through a ripe tomato on the island's counter, the chicken frying on the stove.

She glanced up to see Caleb alone. "Where's the appraiser?" she asked.

"On his way back to Lyndon."

"He wasn't hungry?"

Caleb snagged a chunk of tomato and popped it into his mouth. "He didn't know there was anything on offer."

"You didn't offer to feed him?" It was more than two-and-a-half hours back to Lyndon.

"I didn't think it was worth the risk."

She gave him a perplexed look.

"I don't cook," he clarified.

"Don't be ridiculous." She turned her back on him to flip the last of the tortillas frying in the pan. "Everybody cooks."

"Not me."

She threw the vegetables in with the chicken. "How is that possible? You said you lived alone. Please, don't tell me you have servants."

"I don't have servants. Does anybody have servants in this day and age? I live in a high-rise apartment in downtown Chicago. I'm surrounded by excellent restaurants."

"You eat out every night?" She couldn't imagine it.

"I do a lot of business over dinner," he told her easily. "But most of the restaurants in the area also offer takeout."

"It's hard to believe you survive on takeout." She turned back, returning to chopping the tomato on the island. How could he be so fit eating pizza, burgers and chicken?

"There's takeout. And then there's takeout." He spread his arms and rested the heels of his hands against the lip of the granite countertop, cornerwise from where she worked. "Andre's, around the corner from my apartment, will send up filet mignon, baby potatoes in a sweet dill sauce and primavera lettuce salad with papaya dressing."

Suddenly, her soft-taco recipe seemed lame. She paused. "You must make a lot of money to afford meals like that."

He was silent for a long moment, and she quickly realized her observation had been rude. It was none of her business how much money he made.

"I do okay," he finally allowed.

"Tell me something about your job." She tried to graciously shift the subject.

She also realized she was curious. What had happened to the seventeen-year-old cowboy who landed in Chicago with nothing more than a high school education. It couldn't have been easy for him.

"The company's called Active Equipment." He reached out and snagged another chunk of tomato.

She threatened him with her chopping knife.

But he only laughed. "We sell heavy equipment to construction companies, exploration and resource companies, even ranchers."

"So, like a car dealership?"

"Not a dealership. It's a multinational corporation. We manufacture the equipment before we sell it." With lightning speed, he chose another piece of tomato from the juicy pile and popped it into his mouth, sucking the liquid from the tip of his finger.

"There's not going to be any left for the tacos," she warned.

"I'll risk it."

"So, what do you do at this corporation?"

Caleb swallowed. "I run it."

"What part of it?"

"All of it."

Her hand stilled. "You run an entire corporation?" He'd risen all the way to the top at age twenty-seven? That seemed impossible.

"Yes."

"I don't understand."

He coughed out a laugh. "I'm the president and chief executive officer."

"They gave you *that* many promotions?"

"Not exactly. They let me run things, because they have no choice. I own it."

She set down the knife. She couldn't believe it. "You *own* Active Equipment?"

He nodded.

"How?"

He shrugged. "Hard work, intelligence and a few big financial risks along the way."

"But—"

"You should stop being so surprised that I'm not a loser."

He paused, but she didn't know how to respond to that.

"Though it's true that I can't cook," he allowed with a crooked smile. "I guess I concentrated on the things I was good at and muddled my way through the rest."

"With filet mignon and baby potatoes. Poor you." She kept her tone flippant, but inside she acknowledged he was right. She should stop being so surprised at his accomplishments.

"It wasn't always that way," he told her, tone going more serious. "In the beginning, it was cheap food, a crappy basement suite and two jobs."

Then he straightened his spine, squaring his shoulders. "But I was never coming back here. I'd have starved to death before I'd have come back to Wilton with my tail between my legs."

She found her heart going out to the teenager he'd been back then. "Was it that bad? Were you in danger of starving?"

His posture relaxed again. "No real danger. I was young and healthy. Hard work was good for me. And not even the most demanding bosses could hold a candle to Wilton Terrell."

She retrieved the knife and scraped the tomato chunks from the wooden cutting board into a glass bowl. "So now, you're a self-made man."

"Impressed?"

Mandy wasn't sure how to answer that. Money wasn't everything. "Are you happy?"

"Delirious."

"You have friends? A social life? A girlfriend?" She turned away, crossing the short space to the stove, removing the tortilla shell, setting it on the stack and switching off the burner. She didn't want him to see her expression when he started talking about his girlfriend.

"No girlfriend," he said from behind.

"Why not?" she asked without turning.

"No time, I guess. Never met the right girl."

"You should." She turned back. "Make the time. Meet a nice girl."

His expression went thoughtful, and he regarded her with obvious curiosity. "What about you? Why no boyfriend?"

"Because I'm stuck in the wilds of Colorado ranch country. How am I going to meet a man?"

"Go to Denver. Buy yourself a pretty dress."

She couldn't help glancing down at her simple T-shirt and faded blue jeans with a twinge of self-consciousness. "You don't like my clothes?"

"They're fine for right now, but we're not dancing in a club."

"I've never danced in a real club." A barn, sure, and at the Weasel in Lyndon, but never in a real club.

"Seriously?"

She rolled her eyes at his tone of surprise. "Where would I dance in a club?"

He moved around the island, blue eyes alight with merriment. "If we were in Chicago, I'd dress you up and show you a good time."

"Pretty self-confident, aren't you?" But her pulse had jumped at the thought of dancing with Caleb.

He reached out, lifted one of her hands and twirled her in a spin, pulling her against his body to dance her in the two-step across the kitchen. She reflexively followed his smooth lead.

"Clearly, you've been practicing the Chicago nightlife," she noted.

"Picture mood lighting and a crowd," he whispered in her ear.

"And maybe a band?" she asked, the warmth of his body seeping into her skin, forcing her lungs to work harder to drag in the thickening air.

"You like country?" he asked. "Blues? Jazz? There are some phenomenal jazz clubs in Chicago."

"I'm a country girl," she responded brightly, desperate to mask her growing arousal.

"You'd like jazz," he said with conviction.

The timer pinged for the simmering chicken, and they both halted. Their gazes met, and their breaths mingled.

She could see exactly what he was thinking. "No," she whispered huskily, even though she was definitely feeling it, too. They were not going to let this attraction go over the edge to a kiss.

"Yes," he responded, his fingertips flexing against the small of her back. "But not right now."

Caleb had known it was only a matter of time before Maureen Jacobs, Mandy's mother, extended him some Lyndon Valley hospitality. He wasn't really in a mood for socializing, but he couldn't insult her by saying no to her dinner invitation. So, he'd shut the ranch office computer down early, sighing his disappointment that the listing hadn't come up on the broker's web site yet. Then he drove the rental car over the gravel roads to the Jacobs ranch.

There, he returned friendly hugs, feeling surprisingly at home as he settled in, watching Mandy's efficient movements from the far reaches of the living room in the Jacobs family home. The Jacobses always had the biggest house, the biggest spread and the biggest family in the valley. Caleb couldn't count the number of times he had been here for dinner as a child and a teenager. He, Reed and Travis had all been good friends growing up.

He'd never watched Mandy like this. She had always blended in with her two sisters, little kids in pigtails and scuffed jeans, and was beneath his notice. Now, she was all he could focus on as she flitted from the big, open-concept kitchen to the dining area, chatting with her mother and sister, refilling glasses of iced tea, checking on dishes in the oven and on the stove, while making sure the finishing touches were perfect on the big, rectangular table.

Caleb couldn't imagine the logistics of dinner for seven people every single night. Tonight, one of Mandy's two sisters was here, along with her two brothers, Travis and Seth, who was the oldest. And her parents, Hugo and Maureen, who looked quite a bit older than Caleb had expected, particularly Hugo, who seemed pale and slightly unsteady on his feet.

"I see the way you're looking at my sister," Travis said in an undertone as he took the armchair opposite Caleb in the corner of the living room.

"I was thinking she suits it here," Caleb responded, only half lying. He was thinking a whole lot of other things that were better left unsaid.

"She does," Travis agreed, "but that wasn't what I meant."

"She's a very beautiful woman," Caleb acknowledged. He wasn't going to lie, but he certainly wasn't going to admit the extent of his attraction to Mandy, either.

"Yes, she is." Travis set his glass of iced tea on the small table between them and relaxed back into the overstuffed chair.

Caleb tracked Mandy's progress from the stovetop to the counter, where her mother was busy with a salad, watching as the two of them laughed at something Mandy said. He didn't want to reinforce Travis's suspicions, but his curiosity got the better of him "Did she and Reed ever...?"

Travis shook his head. "It was pretty hard to get close to your brother. He was one bottled up, angry man after you lit out without him."

Caleb felt himself bristle at the implication. He hadn't deserted Reed. He'd begged his brother to come with him. "It wasn't my leaving that did the bottling."

"Didn't help," said Travis.

Caleb hit the man with a warning glare.

"I'm saying he lost his mother, then he lost you, and he was left to cope with your father's temper and crazy expectations all on his own."

Caleb cleared his dry throat with a sip of his own iced tea. "He should have come with me. Left Wilton here to rot."

"You understand why he didn't, don't you?"

"No." Caleb would never understand why Reed had refused to leave.

"Because of your mother."

"I know what he said." But it had never made sense to Caleb.

Their mother was gone. And the legacy of the ranch land didn't mean squat to Caleb. There was nothing but bad memories here for them both. Their father had worked their mother to death on that land.

The sound of female laughter wafted from the kitchen again. Caleb couldn't help but contrast the loud, chaotic scene in this big, family house to his own penthouse apartment with its ultramodern furniture, crisp, cool angles of glass and metal, its silence and order. Everything was always in its place, or at least everything was sitting exactly where he'd last left it.

Maureen passed her husband, Hugo, giving him a quick stroke across the back of the neck. He responded with a secretive smile and a quick squeeze of her hand.

Here was another thing that wasn't in Caleb's frame of reference, relaxed and loving parents. He couldn't remember his mother ever voluntarily touching his father. And his father had certainly never looked at his wife, Sasha, with affection.

Travis shifted his position in the armchair. "Reed thought you were afraid to stay and fight."

Caleb straightened. "Afraid?"

Travis shrugged, indicating he was only the messenger.

"I hated my old man," Caleb clarified. "But I was never afraid of him."

That was a lie, of course. As a child, Caleb had been terrified of his father. Wilton was exacting and demanding, and quick with a strap or the back of his hand. But by the time Caleb was seventeen, he had a good two inches on his father, and he'd have fought back if Wilton had tried anything. Reed was even bigger than Caleb, and Wilton was no physical threat to Reed by then.

"Where do you think Reed went?" Travis asked.

"I couldn't begin to guess," Caleb responded, thinking Reed's decisions were finally his own. He honestly hoped his brother was happy away from here.

He'd thought a lot about it over the past two days. Reed was perfectly entitled to live his life any way he saw fit. As was Caleb, and Caleb had become more and more convinced that selling the ranch was the right thing to do.

Reed could do whatever he wanted with the money. And, in the short term, Caleb was in no position to hang around Lyndon Valley and run things. And he sure couldn't continue to depend on the Jacobses to help him out.

He supposed he could hire a professional ranch manager. But, then what? It wasn't as if he was ever coming back again. And Reed had made his choice by leaving. If Reed had any interest in keeping the ranch, all it would have taken was for him to jot down a contact number in his cryptic note. Caleb would have called, and they could have worked this whole thing out.

Mandy swished across the room, a huge bowl of mashed potatoes in her oven-mitt-covered hands. She'd changed from her usual blue jeans to a pair of gray slacks and a sleeveless, moss-green sweater. It clung to her curves and brought out the color of her eyes. The slacks molded to her rear end, while her rich, chestnut-colored hair flowed like a curtain around her smooth, bare shoulders.

"I see the way you're looking at my sister," Travis repeated.

Caleb glanced guiltily away.

"You hurt her," Travis added, "and we're going to have a problem."

"I have nothing but respect for Mandy," Caleb lied. While he certainly had respect for Mandy, he was also developing a very powerful lust for her.

"This isn't Chicago," Travis warned.

"I'm aware that I'm not in Chicago." Chicago had never been remotely like this.

"We're ready," Maureen announced in a singsong voice.

Mandy sent Caleb a broad smile and motioned him over to the big table. Then she seemed to catch Travis's dark expression, and her eyes narrowed in obvious confusion.

"She's a beautiful, intelligent, strong-minded woman,"

Caleb said to Travis in an undertone. "You should worry about her hurting me."

Travis rose to his feet. "I don't care so much about you. And I'm not likely to take her out behind the barn and knock any sense into her."

Caleb stood to his full height. "Does she know you try to intimidate guys like this?"

The question sent a brief flash of concern across Travis's expression. Caleb tried to imagine Mandy's reaction to Travis's brotherly protectiveness.

It was all Caleb could do not to laugh. "Stalemate."

"I'll still take you out behind the barn."

"I'm not going to hurt Mandy," Caleb promised.

Not that he wouldn't let Mandy make up her own mind about him. She was a grown woman, and if she offered a kiss, he was taking a kiss. If she offered more, well, okay, he didn't imagine he'd be around long enough for that to happen. So there was no sense in borrowing trouble.

He deliberately took a chair across the table from Mandy instead of sitting next to her. Travis grunted his approval.

As dishes were passed around and plates filled up, the family's conversation became free-flowing and boisterous.

"If there's a competing interest lurking out there," Mandy's sister Abigail was saying, "I can't find it. But it's important that as many ranchers as possible show up at the first meeting."

"We need a united front," Hugo put in, helping himself to a slice of roast beef before passing the platter to Travis. "It's suspicious to me that they're calling the review five years early."

"The legislation allows for a water use review anytime after thirty years and before thirty-five," Abigail responded. "Technically, they're not early."

Seth, the eldest brother, stepped in as he reached for a homemade bun. "When was the last time the state government did anything at the *earliest* possible date? Dad's right, there's something they're not telling us."

"I've put in an access to information request," said Abigail. "Maybe that'll solve the mystery."

"That won't get you anything," Hugo grumbled. "The bureaucrats will just stonewall."

"You should catch Caleb up," Mandy suggested.

"This is important to you, too," said Travis, and Caleb waited for him to elaborate.

"Any decrease in the flexibility of our water licenses, will devalue the range land."

"Devalue the range land?" Seth interjected. "Who cares about the land value? It'll impact our grazing density. There are operations up and down the valley that are marginal as it is. The Stevensons, for example. They don't have river access anywhere on their land. A couple of tributaries, but they depend on their wells."

"Seth," Maureen put in, her voice stern. "Did anyone ask you to bring your soapbox to the dinner table?"

Seth's lips thinned for a moment. But then he glanced down at his plate. "Sorry, Mom."

Maureen's face transformed into a friendly smile. "Now, Caleb. How long do you expect to be in Lyndon?"

Caleb swallowed a mouthful of potatoes smothered in the best gravy he'd ever eaten. "A few days. Maybe a week."

"We're sorry you missed the funeral, dear." Maureen's tone was even, but he detected a rebuke. One look at Mandy's expression told him he'd detected correctly.

"I was tied up with work," he said.

"Did you know Caleb owns his own company in Chicago?" Mandy asked.

Caleb appreciated the change in topic, and silently thanked Mandy. The Jacob family would learn soon enough that he was planning to sell the Terrell ranch. Just like everyone would soon learn about Wilton's will. But he was in no hurry to field the inevitable questions.

"Active Equipment," he told them. "Heavy machinery. We're

making inroads into Asia and Canada, and we hope to succeed in the South American market soon."

"That's lovely, dear," said Maureen, her quick gaze going from plate to plate, obviously checking to see if anyone was ready for seconds.

"Active Equipment?" asked Hugo, tone sharp and vaguely accusing. "*The* Active Equipment, loaders and backhoes?"

"Yes," Caleb confirmed.

"So, you can get me a discount?"

Maureen scowled at her husband. Travis laughed, and Mandy's eyes danced with amusement.

"Absolutely," Caleb answered, unable to look away from Mandy. Her green eyes sparkled like emeralds under the chandelier, and he didn't think he'd ever seen a more kissable set of lips. "Just let me know what you need."

"Seth and I will come up with a list," said Hugo.

"Happy to help out," said Caleb.

Mandy's lashes swept briefly down over her eyes, and the tip of her tongue moistened her lower lip. He didn't dare glance Travis's way.

Three

Mandy couldn't help but stare at the tall, elegant, brunette woman standing on the porch of the Terrell ranch house. She wore a chic, textured, taupe jacket, with black piping along the neck, lapels and faux pockets. It had a matching, straight skirt, and the ensemble was layered over a black, lace camisole. Her black, leather pumps were high heeled, closed toed with an open weave along the outsides.

Her earrings were large—a woven, copper geometric pattern that dangled beneath short, stylishly cut hair. Her makeup was subtle, coral lips, soft thick lashes, sculpted brows and dusky shadow that set off her dark, hazel eyes. She held a black, rhinestone purse tucked under one arm, and a leather briefcase in the opposite hand.

How she'd made it to the porch dust-free was beyond Mandy.

"Can I help you with something?" Mandy belatedly asked.

"I'm looking for Caleb Terrell." The woman's voice was crisp and businesslike.

"I'm afraid he's not here at the moment."

The woman's lips compressed in obvious impatience.

"Was he expecting you?" Mandy asked, confused and curious in equal measure.

"*I* was expecting *him*. Two days ago in Chicago." The woman clearly had a close enough relationship with Caleb that she had expectations, and she was free to express frustration if he didn't meet them.

A girlfriend? A lover? He'd said he had none, but evidence to the contrary was standing right here in front of Mandy.

"Would you like to come in?" she offered, remembering her manners, telling herself Caleb's personal life was none of her business. "He should be back anytime."

Sure, he'd made a couple of flirtatious allusions in their conversations. But they were harmless. He hadn't even kissed her. She certainly hadn't taken any of it seriously.

The woman smiled, transforming her face, and she held out a slim, perfectly manicured hand. "Forgive me. I'm Danielle Marin."

Mandy hesitated only a brief second before holding out her own, blunt-nailed, tanned and slightly callused hand.

She couldn't help but wish she was wearing something other than a plain, blue cotton blouse and faded jeans. There was some eyelet detail on the collar, and at least she didn't have manure on her boots. Then again, she'd been sweating in the barn all morning, and her casual ponytail was certainly the worse for wear.

"Mandy Jacobs," she introduced herself. "I'm, uh. I've been helping out on the ranch."

"I'm sure Caleb appreciates that." Danielle waved a hand in the air as she stepped into the house. "I have to say, this whole situation borders on the ridiculous."

Mandy closed the door behind them. She couldn't disagree. "Once we find Reed, things will smooth out."

"Any progress on that?" Danielle asked, setting her purse on the side table in the entryway and parking her briefcase beneath. "Caleb told me you were spearheading the effort."

Mandy didn't know what to say to that. She didn't want to share details with a stranger, but she couldn't very well ask about Danielle's relationship with Caleb without being rude.

Danielle strolled her way into the great room, gazing at the high ceiling and the banks of windows overlooking the river. "I assume you've already checked his usual hotels."

Mandy followed. "Reed never traveled much. But I have checked hotels, hospitals and with the police as far away as Fort Collins."

"Car-rental agencies?"

"He took a ranch truck."

Danielle nodded. "Have you tried checking his credit-card activity?"

Mandy tried to figure out if Danielle was joking. Judging by her expression, she was serious.

"I wouldn't know how to do that," Mandy said slowly. Was she even allowed to do that? It sounded like it might be illegal.

"It's not a service we could provide, but I do have some contacts..." Danielle let the offer hang.

Mandy didn't know what to say. Was Danielle suggesting she could help Mandy break the law?

The front door opened, and a pair of boots sounded in the entryway. Mandy took a couple of steps back and crooked her head to confirm it was Caleb. Thank goodness.

He gazed quizzically at her expression as he strode down the short hall. Then, at the living-room entrance, he halted in his tracks. "Danielle?"

"Yes," Danielle answered shortly as she moved in on him.

"What on earth are you doing in Colorado?"

"What on earth are *you* still doing in Colorado?"

"I told you it was going to take a few days."

"That was a few days ago."

"*Two* days ago."

"Do you want this to work or not?"

Mandy scooted toward the kitchen, determined to get away from the private conversation. One thing was sure, if Caleb kept flirting with other women, his relationship with Danielle was definitely not going to work out.

"We have to be in Sao Paulo by the sixteenth," Danielle's voice carried to the kitchen. "We've made a commitment. There's no cancellation insurance on this kind of deal, Caleb."

"Have I done something to make you think I'm stupid?" Caleb asked.

Mandy wasn't proud of it, but her feet came to a halt the moment she was around the corner in the kitchen, intense curiosity keeping her tuned to what was happening in the living room.

"You mean, other than moving to Colorado?" Danielle asked.

"I haven't moved to Colorado."

There was a moment of silence, and Mandy found herself straining to hear.

"You have to come back, Caleb."

"I can't leave yet."

"You said you were going to sell."

"I am going to sell."

Mandy was forced to bite back a protest. For years, she'd fantasized about the two brothers reconciling, and they were so close right now. Whatever hard feelings were between them, she was confident they loved each other. And they were the only family each of them had.

"You can look at offers just as easily from Chicago," said Danielle.

"And who runs the ranch until then?"

"What about that Mandy woman?"

"She's doing me a favor just by being here." There was another pause. "Mandy?" Caleb called. "Where did you go?"

"Kitchen," she responded, quickly busying herself at the counter. "You two want coffee?"

"You don't need to make us coffee," Caleb called back.

"It's no problem."

She heard him approach.

Then his footfalls crossed the kitchen, his voice lowering as he arrived behind her. "You *don't* need to make us coffee."

She didn't turn around. "You and your girlfriend should sit down and—"

"My *girlfriend?*"

"Talk this out," Mandy finished. "But, can I say, I really hope you'll give it some time before you sell, Caleb, because I know Reed—"

Caleb wrapped a big hand around her upper arm and turned her to face him. "She's not my girlfriend."

"Oh." Then what was she doing here? Why were they making plans for a vacation in Brazil?

"She's my financial lawyer."

"Sure." Whatever. It didn't mean they weren't romantically involved.

He lowered his voice further. "And why did your mind immediately go to a romance?"

"Because she's gorgeous," Mandy offered, counting on her finger. "Because she's here. Because she just told you if you didn't come back to Chicago, things weren't going to work out between you."

Caleb's voice lowered to a hiss. "And what exactly do you think I've been doing with you?"

She was slow to answer, because she really wasn't sure what the heck he'd been doing with her. "A harmless flirtation. I assumed you didn't mean it the way—"

"I did."

"I'd love some coffee," came Danielle's sultry voice from the kitchen doorway.

"Coming up." Mandy quickly turned away from Caleb.

"She thinks you and I are dating," he said to Danielle in a clear voice.

Danielle's response was a melodic laugh. "Like I'd get you to sit still long enough for a date."

"See?" Caleb finished before backing off.

"I'm setting up a corporation for him in Brazil," Danielle

explained. "Do you by any chance have an internet connection? A scanner?"

"In the office," Caleb answered. "Up the stairs, first door on the right."

When Mandy turned around, two stoneware mugs of coffee in her hand, Danielle was gone.

Caleb was standing in front of the table in the breakfast nook. "I'm not dating her."

"Got that." Mandy took a determined step forward, ignoring the undercurrents from their rather intimate conversation. "Brazil?"

"It's a huge, emerging market."

She set the two mugs down on the table. "Are you, like a billionaire?"

"I've never stopped to do the math."

"But you might be." No wonder he could give up the ranch without a second thought. He wasn't quite the philanthropist he made himself out to be.

"The net worth of a corporation is irrelevant. All the money's tied up in the business. Even if you did want to know the value, you'd spend months wading your way through payables, receivables, inventory, assets and debts to find an answer. And by the time you found it, the answer would have changed."

"But you don't need the money from the ranch," was really Mandy's point.

Caleb drew a sigh. "I'm giving the money to Reed because he earned it." Caleb's hand tightened around the back of one of the chairs. "Boy, did he earn it."

"Then don't sell the ranch."

"I can't stay here and run it."

Mandy tried to stay detached, but her passion came through in the pleading note of her voice. "Reed doesn't want the money. He wants the ranch."

"Then, where is he?"

"He's sulking."

Caleb gave a cold laugh. "At least you've got that right. He's off somewhere, licking his wounds, mired in the certain and self-righteous anger that I'm about to cheat him out of his inheritance. Nice."

"Reed doesn't trust easily."

"You think?"

"And you've been gone a long time."

"When I left, I *begged* him to come with me."

"Well, he didn't. And you have a choice here. You can make things better or you can make them worse."

"No. Reed had a choice here." Caleb's voice was implacable. "He could have stayed."

"He'll be back."

Caleb shook his head. "I don't think so. And he'll be better off with the money, anyway. He can go wherever he wants, do whatever he wants. He'll be free of this place forever."

"If he wanted to be free," she offered reasonably, "he'd have left with you in the first place."

Caleb's eyes narrowed. "Why do you want him back here so badly?"

Mandy wasn't sure how to answer the question. What she wanted was for Caleb and Reed to reconcile. She wanted the ranch to stay in the Terrell family for Reed's children, for Sasha's grandchildren. Reed had sacrificed ten years to protect his heritage. Caleb had no business pulling it out from under him.

Caleb watched the last of the dozen pieces of paper disappear into the ranch house office fax machine. The machine emitted a series of beeps and buzzes that indicated the pages were successfully reaching the Lyndon real-estate office.

"You did it, didn't you?" Mandy's accusing voice came from the office doorway. It was full dark, and the ranch yard lights outside the window mingled with the glow of the desk lamp and the stream of illumination from the upstairs hallway. Danielle had retired to the guest room half an hour ago. Caleb thought Mandy had already left.

"The Terrell Cattle Company is officially for sale," he replied, swiping the pages from the cache tray and straightening them into a neat pile.

"You're making a mistake," said Mandy.

"It's my mistake to make."

She moved into the room. "Did you ever stop to wonder why he did it?"

"Reed or Wilton?"

"Your father."

Caleb nodded. "I did. For about thirty-six hours straight. I called Reed half a dozen times after I left my lawyer's office that day. I thought he might have some answers. But he didn't call back. And eventually his voice-mail box was full and I knew it was hopeless."

"Danielle's office?"

"Different lawyer."

"Oh."

Caleb set down the papers and turned to prop himself against the lip of the desk. "I guessed maybe Reed and the old man had a fight, and leaving me the ranch was Wilton's revenge."

"They had about a thousand fights."

Caleb gave a cold chuckle. "Wilton fought with me, too. A guy couldn't do anything right when it came to my old man. If you piled the manure to the right, he wanted it to the left. You used the plastic manure fork, you should have used the metal one. You started brushing from the front of the horse, you should have started from the back—" He stopped himself. Just talking about it made his stomach churn. How the hell Reed had put up with it for ten extra years was beyond Caleb. The guy deserved a medal.

"My theory," said Mandy, moving farther into the dimly lit room, "is that once you were gone, he forgot you were such a failure." An ironic smile took the sting out of her words.

"While Reed was still here to keep screwing up over and over again?"

"Got a better theory?"

"He found my corporation thanks to Google and decided I was worth a damn?" Even as he said the words, Caleb knew it was impossible. He'd spent the better part of his adult life warning himself not to look for his father's approval. There was nothing down that road but bitter disappointment.

Mandy perched herself on the inset, cushioned window seat. She was silhouetted now by the lights from the yard. "You have to know you are worth a damn."

"You're too kind."

"Reed's worth a damn, too."

"No argument from me."

She tucked her feet up onto the wide, bench seat, and he noticed she was wearing whimsical sky-blue-and-pale-pink, mottled socks. It surprised him. Made her seem softer somehow, more vulnerable.

"I don't understand why you're in such a rush to sell," she said.

"That's because you live in the Lyndon Valley and not in Chicago."

"Rash decisions are compulsory in Chicago?"

He moved across the room and took the opposite end of the bench, angling his body toward her and bracing his back against the wall, deciding there was no reason not to give her an explanation. "I've had two weeks to think about it."

"Reed had ten years."

"In many ways, so did I."

Mandy shifted her position, smoothing her loose hair back from her face. His gaze hungrily followed her motion.

"Did you ever wish you'd stayed?"

He hesitated at the unsettling question, not sure how to answer. Back then, he'd second-guessed himself for months, even years, over leaving Reed. But it all came down to Wilton. "He killed my mother," Caleb said softly. "I couldn't reward him for that."

"She died of pneumonia."

"Because it was left untreated. Because she was terrified of telling him she was sick. Because he would have berated and belittled her for her weakness. Terrells are not weak."

"I never thought you were."

"I'm not," he spat, before he realized it wasn't Mandy he was angry with.

She tossed back her hair. "Reed wasn't weak. Yet, he stayed."

"He squared it in his head somehow."

Reed claimed he wanted to protect his mother's heritage, since half the ranch had belonged to her family. Which, looking back, was obviously the reason Wilton had married her. The man was incapable of love.

"She was twenty years younger than him," Caleb remembered. "Did you know that?"

"I knew she was younger. I didn't know by how much. I remember thinking she was beautiful." Mandy's voice became introspective. "I remember wishing I could be that beautiful."

Caleb couldn't hold back his opinion. "You are that beautiful."

Mandy laughed. "No, I'm not." She held out her hands. "Calluses. I have calluses. Danielle has a perfect French manicure, and I have calluses." She peered at her small hands. "I think there might even be dirt under my fingernails."

"Danielle has never had to clean tack."

"No kidding."

"I mean, she lives a completely different life than you do."

Mandy's face twisted into a grimace. "She goes to parties and I shovel manure?"

"Her world is all about image. Yours is all about practicality."

"I'm just a sturdy, little workhorse, aren't I?"

"Are you wallowing in self-pity, Mandy Jacobs?"

She went silent, her glare speaking for her.

Caleb moved inches closer, fighting a grin of amusement. "Are you by any chance jealous of Danielle?"

Mandy tossed back her hair in defiance. "Jealous of a stunningly beautiful, elegant, intelligent, successful lawyer, who's flying off to Rio—"

"Sao Paulo," Caleb corrected, enjoying the flash of emotion that appeared deep within Mandy's green eyes.

"They're both in Brazil."

"It's a big country. One's a beach resort, the other's full of skyscrapers, banks and boardrooms." He fought the urge to reach out and touch her. "But I'd take you to Rio if that's where you wanted to go."

She cocked her head sideways. "You'd take me to Rio?"

"I would." He dared stroke an index finger across the back of her hand. "We'd dress up, and go dancing at a real club and have blender drinks on the beach. You could even get a manicure if you'd like."

"Are you flirting with me?"

He met her gaze full on. "Absolutely."

"You have women like Danielle in your life, and yet you're flirting with me?"

"I am."

"Why?"

Caleb debated for a moment before answering. But then he reminded himself he was in Colorado. People were forthright around here. And he owed Mandy no less than she was giving him.

"Because you're real," he told her. "You're not some plastic package, constructed to appeal to a man's anthropological triggers. When you laugh, it's because you're happy. When you argue, it's because you have a point to make. And when your eyes smolder, it's because you're attracted to me, not because you've spent days and weeks practicing the exact, right look to make a man think you're interested in him."

"I'm not interested in you."

"But you are." He smoothed a stray lock of her hair and tucked it behind one ear. "That's what's so amazing about you. Your body language doesn't lie."

"And if my body language slaps you across the face?"

"I hope it'll be because I've done something to deserve it." Because, then the slap would be worth it.

"You're impossible." But her voice had gone bedroom husky. Her pupils were dilated, and her dark pink lips were softened, slightly parted.

"It's not me you're fighting," he told her.

She didn't answer. Her breathing grew deeper while a pink flush stained her cheeks.

He moved the last couple of inches. Then he dared to bracket her face with his hands. Her skin was smooth, warm and soft against his palms. His pulse jumped, desire igniting a buzz deep in his belly.

He bent his head forward, his lips parting in anticipation of her taste. He hadn't even kissed her yet, and desire was turning his bloodstream into a tsunami.

She sucked in a quick breath, her jade-green eyes fluttering closed.

Caleb could tell stop signals from go signals, and this was definitely a go. Her head tilted sideways, as she leaned into his palm. He crossed the final inches, her sweet breath puffing against his face in the split second before his lips touched hers.

Desire exploded in his chest. He'd meant it to be a gentle kiss, but raw passion pushed him forward.

He'd known it would be good, guessed she would taste like ambrosia, but nothing had prepared him for the rush of raw lust that made his arms wrap around her and his entire body harden to steel.

He opened his mouth, deepening the kiss. She whimpered in surrender, giving him access, her small tongue parrying with his, while his broad palm stroked its way from her waist to her hip, to the curve at the side of her breast.

He shifted his body, pulling her into his lap, never breaking the kiss as her soft, pert behind settled against him. He raked the satin of her hair out of the way, his fingertips convulsing against her scalp. Her small hands clung to his shoulders, hanging on tight, while her rounded breasts pressed erotically against his chest.

He wanted to rip off her clothes, push her back on the seat, or down on the floor, and ravage her body until neither of them could see straight. He knew he couldn't do that, knew he was losing control, knew he had to drag them back to reality before their passion got completely out of control.

But then her hot hands slid the length of his chest, and he put sanity on hold. She freed the buttons of his cotton shirt, her palms searing into his bare skin.

His hand closed over her breast, feeling its weight through the fabric of her shirt and the lace of her bra. He kissed her harder, deeper, settling her more firmly on the heat of his need. Her kisses trailed to his chest, over his pecs, across one flat nipple, and he groaned in reaction.

"We can't," he whispered harshly, even as he buried his face in her fragrant hair and prayed she'd keep going.

She stilled, her breath cooling a damp spot on his bare skin.

They were both silent for a long moment, while Caleb tried unsuccessfully to bring his emotions under control.

"I'm sorry," she whispered, lips grazing his skin.

"Are you kidding me?" he breathed. He forced himself to draw back, tipping up her chin and gazing into her passion-clouded eyes. "I have never—"

The cell phone in her jeans pocket buzzed, startling them both.

"—ever," he continued, trying to hold her gaze, reluctant to let the moment go.

The cell phone buzzed again.

"Fortuitous?" she asked, seeming to regain her equilibrium.

"Not the word I would have used." He sighed.

She shifted off his lap, slipping her hand into her jeans pocket to retrieve the cell phone.

"Abigail," she announced while she pressed the talk button. "Hey, Abby."

Caleb couldn't believe she could sound so normal. He sure wasn't that capable of turning on a dime like that. Desire was still pulsing its way through his extremities. It was going to be long minutes before he would be able to do anything more than breathe.

"When?" Mandy asked into the phone, her voice going guttural.

Her gaze locked on to Caleb's, fear shooting through her irises. "I don't—"

She swayed on her feet, and he instantly leaped to his, holding her steady.

"Where?" she asked hoarsely, bracing herself by grasping his arm. "Yes. Of course." She nodded reflexively. "Yes."

She was silent for another moment, her hand squeezing his arm in a vice grip. "Right now," she told her sister. "I'll be there. Bye." Her tone was whispered as she lowered the phone.

"What?" Caleb prompted, his stomach clenching hard. Something had obviously gone terribly wrong.

"My dad," she managed, blinking back twin pools of gathering tears. "They think it was a stroke."

"Is he…" Caleb couldn't finish the sentence.

"The medical airlift is on its way."

"How bad?"

"Numbness, speech problems, confusion." She broke away from Caleb's hold. "I have to get home."

"I'll drive you."

"No, I can—"

"I'll *drive* you." There wasn't a chance in hell he was letting her speed down the dark, dirt ranch road all alone.

Four

All the lights were blazing when Mandy and Caleb drove up to the ranch house. Caleb's rented SUV had barely come to a halt when she flung open her door, feet barely touching the dirt driveway as she sprinted across the porch. She rushed through the entry hall to the big living room.

There, she saw Seth first, his strong face pinched in concern where he sat on the sofa, holding her mother's hand. Her sister Abby was furiously hitting keys on the computer, while Travis paced in the middle of the room, obviously ready for action and obviously frustrated because there was nothing he could do to help.

"Mom." Mandy rushed forward, sliding down beside her mother and wrapping an arm around her slim shoulders. Her mother's face was pale, eyes red-rimmed and hollow looking.

"The helicopter left about five minutes ago," said Seth.

"They said there wasn't room for Mom." Travis sounded angry.

Mandy heard Caleb enter the house and cross the foyer behind her, but she didn't turn. She felt guilty for being attracted to him, guilty for kissing him, guilty as sin for getting lost in his embrace while her father fell ill and collapsed.

"I'm trying to find her a ticket out of Lyndon for the morning," Abigail put in.

"They're taking him straight to Denver," said Travis. "There's a specialist there, a whole team with the latest technology for early stroke intervention."

"That sounds good," Mandy said to her mother, rubbing Maureen's shoulder with her palm.

"Damn it. The connection is bogged down again," said Abigail.

Caleb stepped fully into the room. "My corporate jet's on the tarmac in Lyndon."

Everyone turned to stare at him.

Seth came to his feet. "How many of us can you take?"

"As many as need to go." He captured Mandy's gaze for a long second.

"I'll stay here," Travis put in, drawing everyone's attention. He glanced at his siblings. "I'm probably the least help there, but I'm the most help here."

Seth nodded his agreement with the suggestion.

Responding to Seth's concurrence, Caleb pulled out his cell phone. "I'll have the pilots meet us at the airport. Mandy, why don't you put together an overnight bag for your mother?"

Abby swiveled back to the computer. "I'm booking a hotel for us in Denver."

"See if there's an Emerald Chateau near the hospital," said Caleb as he pressed the buttons on his phone. "We have a corporate account. Call them and use my name." He put his cell phone to his ear and turned toward the foyer.

Mandy squeezed her mother's cool hand. "Did you hear that, Mom?"

Maureen gave a small nod of acknowledgment.

"Good." Mandy struggled to keep her voice even. Breaking down right now wouldn't help anyone, least of all her mother. "I'm going to pack you a few things. You just sit tight."

"He couldn't speak." Maureen's voice was paper dry, her hand squeezing Mandy's. "He tried, but his words were all muddled. Syllables sometimes, then nonsense."

Mandy swallowed the lump in her throat. "I think that's really common with a stroke. And it's sounds like they've got a great team in Denver. He'll get the best care." Her gaze met her brother Seth's and he motioned with his head for her to go pack.

She nodded in response, gently releasing her mother's hand. The sooner they got to Denver, the better.

As she headed for the staircase, she passed Caleb in the foyer, where he was talking on the phone to his pilot. "Two hours, tops," he said. "Right. We'll be there."

She stopped and turned back, reaching out to lay the flat of her hand on his chest, mouthing the words "Thank you."

He placed his hand over hers and gave one quick squeeze then pointed her toward the staircase.

Mandy had never been on a private plane. The flight to Denver was, thankfully, quick and smooth. The Active Equipment jet had room for eight passengers, and Caleb had arranged for a car to take them directly from the airport to the hospital. There, Mandy's mother was the only person allowed to see her father, and the nurse would let her into his room for only a few minutes.

The doctors were medicating him and monitoring him closely to watch for additional strokes. They told the family they needed to keep him calm. The initial prognosis was for a slow, potentially limited recovery. There was no way to tell how much of his speech and mobility he would regain. A doctor told them the first few days were critical.

Although Abby had booked regular rooms at the Denver Emerald Chateau, a word from Caleb to the front-desk clerk had Mandy, Abby and her mother in a luxurious, two-bedroom suite. Caleb and Seth had taken an identical suite at the opposite end of the twentieth-floor hallway.

It was nearly three in the morning before Mandy's mother finally got to bed. Thankfully, she fell asleep almost immediately, and Mandy joined Abby, Seth and Caleb in the suite's living room.

Abigail was handing Seth her cell phone. "Your brother wants to talk to you."

"Thanks, tons." Seth scowled as he accepted the phone.

The only vacant seat was on a small couch next to Caleb, and Mandy sat down. She felt his gaze on her profile, swore she could feel his energy through her pores, but she didn't turn.

"Must we do this *now?*" Seth was asking into the phone.

Mandy gave her sister a quizzical look.

"Seth was talking about dropping out of the Lyndon mayoralty race," Abby explained. "Travis disagrees."

Mandy disagreed, as well, strenuously. Her oldest brother had been planning this political move for over two years. "It'll be weeks before he even needs to campaign."

Abigail huffed as she crossed her arms over her chest. "That's what I told him. And that's what Travis's telling him."

Mandy shook her head. "Dad won't want him to drop out."

Their father had been totally supportive of Seth's decision to run for mayor. The ranching community was slowly being pushed out of the economic framework of the district as tourism operations and small businesses moved in and began to lobby for their own interests.

"Who's going to run the place?" Seth demanded into the phone. "You?"

He listened for a moment, then gave a cold laugh. "Don't make promises you can't keep."

Caleb leaned toward Mandy. "This is a terrible time for them to have this conversation. They have absolutely no perspective at all."

She knew he was right and nodded her agreement. They were all exhausted and their emotions were raw.

Caleb rose to his feet. He moved in front of Seth and motioned for him to hand over the phone. Seth scowled at him, but Caleb persisted. When Seth finally complied, Caleb put the phone to his ear.

"Travis? It's Caleb. You need to go to bed. So does Seth and so do your sisters."

There was a pause.

"In the morning. No. You listen. I don't care who started it. I'm the only one here who's not operating on grief and fear, and I'm telling you to shut it down."

Caleb paused again. "Yes. I will." His gaze slid to Mandy for a brief second. "Of course not."

Abigail rose from her chair to lean over and give Mandy a quick hug. "I'm beat," she whispered in Mandy's ear. "Mind if I use the bathroom first?"

"Go ahead." Mandy squeezed her sister tight, grateful to have her siblings close to her tonight.

"We're going to have to call Katrina in the morning." Abigail referred to their youngest sister who lived in New York City.

"It's almost morning there now," said Mandy.

"When we get up is soon enough. I'm sure it'll be early."

"Yeah," Mandy agreed on a sigh. It was going to be a long day tomorrow.

Abigail made her way to the second bedroom and its en suite bathroom.

Caleb put the cell phone on the coffee table.

Seth rose. "I'm ordering a single malt from room service," he told Caleb. "You want one?"

"Yeah," said Caleb. "I'm right behind you."

Mandy came to her feet to give her oldest brother a big hug.

"You okay?" he whispered gruffly in her ear, ruffling her hair.

"I'll let you know in the morning." Mandy dreaded having him leave the suite, having her sister fall asleep, leaving her alone with her thoughts and fears. She wasn't going to sleep. Her family had just turned on a dime. She had no idea what would come next.

Seth shut the door behind him, and Caleb turned to her. "You're not okay."

"I'm not okay," she agreed, her body turning into one big ache. He stepped closer. "Anything I can do to help?"

"You already have." She drew a shuddering breath, trying to put the night's events in some sort of order. "You have a jet?"

"Active Equipment has a jet."

"But you own Active Equipment."

"True enough."

"Thank you for bringing us all here. I know my mom was terrified…" She swallowed, her throat going raw all over again. "I was so afraid he'd die before—"

Caleb drew her into his strong arms, cradling her against his body. "Of course you were. But he didn't. And you're here now. And there may very well be good news in the morning."

Mandy found herself lying her cheek against Caleb's chest, taking comfort in the steady thud of his heartbeat and the deep, soothing rumble of his voice.

He leaned in and kissed her gently on the temple, bringing all her earlier feelings rushing back. She felt off balance, out of sync, like she was floating in space without a lifeline.

"Caleb," she stuttered. "What we—"

"Shh. Not now. Nothing matters right now."

She closed her eyes. "Are you always this nice?"

"I'm hardly ever this nice." He paused. "You need to sleep now."

"I know." She wished she could lie down right there, right then and stay safe in Caleb's arms for the rest of the night. Deep down inside, she knew she was being foolish. She was emotional and vulnerable, and he seemed strong and safe. It was that simple.

These feelings would probably go away by morning, but right now, they were powerfully strong.

The next morning did bring positive news. Caleb was surprised, along with everyone else, by Hugo's rapid progress.

Hugo recognized all the family members. They were each allowed to visit him, and he was able to say Maureen's name, along with several other rudimentary words, enough to get his general meaning across. His meaning, Caleb noted, was that Seth should continue to plan his campaign for the mayoralty race, Abigail should stay in Denver with Maureen, while Mandy should go home and run the ranch with Travis.

Caleb had to admire the tough old man. Less than twenty-four hours after the stroke, Hugo was regaining movement in his right arm, and he also had some movement in his right foot and ankle. The doctors were very pleased with his progress and feeling optimistic about his eventual recovery, although they cautioned it would take weeks, possibly months.

Seth decided to stay in Denver for some political meetings, so Caleb and Mandy returned alone on the Active Equipment jet. Once in Lyndon, they exited down the airplane staircase and onto the tarmac outside a small maintenance building at the private area of the apron. It was late afternoon, and thick clouds were gathering as the sun made its descent and the air cooled down.

Caleb switched on his cell phone, and Mandy did the same. Hers immediately rang, and they picked up their pace to get away from the sound of the airplane engines.

She plugged one ear and called "hello" just as Caleb's phone rang. They made it around the end of the building, blocking the noise.

Caleb answered his phone with one hand, unlocking and swinging open the chain-link gate with the other. There were few cars in the parking area.

"It's Travis," came the voice at the other end.

"Just touched down in Lyndon," Caleb offered. "Did you talk to your mother?"

"Just got off with her," said Travis. "Dad's progress is still good. The doctors are amazed."

"Good to hear." With his free hand, Caleb hit the unlock button on his key fob and opened the passenger door first.

Mandy was focused on her own conversation as she absently accepted his offer and climbed inside.

"About Danielle," Travis continued.

"Were you able to reach her?" Caleb had tried Danielle's cell this morning and got her voice mail. Odds were good that she'd headed back to Chicago and was on an airplane. Still, he'd asked Travis to retry the call and check the ranch just in case. He'd rushed off so fast last night, he'd barely had time to explain. Danielle wasn't the most patient woman in the world.

"I drove up to your place," Travis confirmed.

"So, she's on her way back to Chicago?"

"Not exactly."

"She's not?" Caleb swung into the driver's seat and slid the key into the ignition.

"You know that hairpin turn where you come out at Joe Mountain?"

"What?"

"Where the rear wheels always break loose?"

Uh-oh. Caleb didn't like where this was going. "Is Danielle all right?"

"She's fine. Now."

"Give me the bad news."

Travis confirmed Caleb's fears. "She couldn't recover from the slide, missed the turn. Got stuck at the edge of the pond. She wasn't hurt, but evidently, there's no cell service at that particular spot."

Caleb groaned and thudded his head on the steering wheel. Mandy spared him a glance of confusion.

"How long was she stuck?" he asked Travis.

"A few hours. I have to give the girl points for moxie. She spotted the Eldridge barn and decided they might be able to help her."

"That barn's seventy years old. And it's half a mile from the road."

"Hard to judge, I guess. Miss Danielle may want to have

her distance vision checked. She climbed through the barbed-wire fence and started hiking."

Caleb groaned again.

"Didn't go well," Travis confirmed. "Apparently you owe her for a designer blazer that got torn. Oh, also the shoes that weren't made for hiking."

"Did she make it to the barn?"

"Barely. By the time she realized it was a derelict, a herd of cattle had cut her off from her car. I guess a bull made some threatening moves, and she ended up climbing into the loft. It's dusty up there and, apparently, there are quite a few spiders."

Caleb shouldn't laugh. He really shouldn't. "I'm in a lot of trouble, aren't I?"

"Hell, yeah. You and me both."

"Why you? I assume you rescued her."

"By the time I got there, she'd been trapped for a few hours."

"Do I by any chance need a new lawyer?"

"She was pretty desperate for a restroom."

Caleb rewhacked his head. Anything less than marble fixtures was considered slumming it for Danielle.

"I told her to go behind the barn," said Travis with an obviously suppressed chuckle.

"Are you laughing?"

"You also owe her for a pair of designer undies. There were nettles."

"Could you just shoot me?"

Mandy had finished her call, twisted her body in the passenger seat and was now staring unabashedly at Caleb.

Caleb met her curious gaze.

"We had to tow her car back with a tractor," said Travis. "Scooter says it needs parts. Hey, can you stop by the auto-parts store while you're in Lyndon?"

"Sure," Caleb agreed fatalistically.

"We'll text you a list."

Caleb braced himself. "She doing okay?"

"She's been in the upstairs bathroom for two hours. I don't

know what women do in there, but hopefully it'll improve her disposition."

"Hopefully," Caleb agreed, but he wasn't holding his breath. "Thanks, Travis."

"No need to thank me. That was the best entertainment I've had all month."

"Don't tell her that."

"Already did. See you, Caleb."

Caleb signed off, pocketing his phone.

"Were you talking to Abigail?" he asked Mandy.

She nodded. "The news on Dad just gets better and better. I'm *so* relieved."

"Good to hear," Caleb agreed.

"You were talking to Travis?" she asked him in return, raising her brows in a prompt.

"Danielle had some car trouble."

"She's still in Colorado?" Mandy was obviously surprised by the news. "I got the impression she was going to be on the first flight out."

"They're sending us a list of parts for the car." Caleb turned the ignition key and started the Escalade.

"Is she okay?"

"She's fine. Travis helped her out. But she's frustrated to be stuck in Lyndon."

His phone rang again, but he didn't recognize the number. He flipped it open. "Caleb Terrell."

"Mr. Terrell? It's Frank Cummings here, Mountain Real Estate. I have some good news for you."

"Hello, Frank."

"We have an interested buyer."

"This soon?" Caleb was surprised. It had been less than twenty-four hours since he'd listed the ranch.

"The gentleman has been watching for opportunities in the area, and he'll be in Lyndon tonight. I'm meeting him for dinner. I was wondering if we might touch base with you by phone in a couple of hours? If all goes well, we'll want to arrange a viewing."

"I'm in Lyndon."

"Right now?"

"Right now."

"Then you should join us for dinner." Frank sounded excited at the prospect.

"Sure." Why not? If it was a serious buyer, Caleb would like to look him in the eye and make his pitch. "I'm with someone," he told Frank, his glance going to Mandy.

"Up to you, but feel free to bring them along."

"Where and when?"

"Riverfront Grill at six."

"We'll be there." He ended the call.

Mandy arched a brown. "We'll be where?"

He pocketed his phone and pulled the shifter into Reverse. "Is there any chance I can trust you?"

Mandy buckled up. "To do what?"

"To behave yourself—"

She sputtered an unintelligible protest.

"Frank Cummings has a buyer," he finished.

She froze, jaw dropping. "For the ranch?"

He reversed the SUV out of the parking spot, tires slipping to a stop on the gravel scattered on top of the pavement. Then he shifted into Drive. "Only thing I'm selling."

"But… You… That's too fast!"

"I don't think there are any speed regulations."

"Who's the buyer? What does he want? Is he going to keep it as a working ranch?"

Caleb shot her a look of annoyance. "You can't ask him questions like that. It's none of our business."

She clenched her jaw.

"I mean it, Mandy. If you come to dinner, you have to behave yourself."

"You make me sound like a child."

"You're about as emotional as one."

"Can you blame me? Really, Caleb. Can you blame me for trying to protect your land and your family—"

"It's not yours to protect."

"—from someone so determined to make such a stupid mistake?"

"You're referring to me?"

"If the shoe fits."

He glanced sternly at her one more time. "You want to come to this dinner, or not? I'm serious, Mandy. I don't want to dump you off on the side of the road, but I'm not taking a lit stick of dynamite into a business meeting."

She seemed to have to think about it for a moment.

He waited.

"I won't ask him his plans for the ranch," she finally promised, folding her hands primly on her lap, staring straight ahead and looking for all the world like a mischievous young girl.

He squelched an urge to waggle his finger at her. "You are to say nothing but cheerful, positive things about Terrell Ranch and the Lyndon Valley."

She turned to him, tone dripping with sarcasm. "I *love* the Lyndon Valley."

"And if you could do that little pouty thing with your mouth, make the guy think he'll have a sexy, farmer's daughter living next door—"

Mandy socked Caleb soundly in the shoulder. "Watch your mouth."

"I'd rather watch yours."

"And you're worried about *my* behavior?"

He cracked a grin. "I'll be good if you will."

And then he found himself second-guessing the wisdom of that particular promise. Honestly, it might be worth letting her blow the sale if it meant they could flirt instead.

Five

At a window table at the Riverfront Grill, Mandy plucked the cherry from the top of her hot-fudge sundae. She considered it consolation food, since Caleb's sales meeting was going so well. Frank Cummings had come prepared with everything from surveyors' drawings to photographs and climate charts. Nathan Brooks, a fifty-something man from Colorado Springs, was enthusiastic and obviously interested in the ranch.

She licked the whipped cream from the cherry and popped the fruit into her mouth, catching Caleb's gaze as she chewed contemplatively and swallowed.

"I'm sorry?" Caleb turned his attention back to Nathan. "Can you repeat the question?"

"The upkeep of the house?"

"Has been regular, thorough maintenance, from paint and fixtures to plumbing and electrical."

Mandy selected one of the dessert spoons. The waiter had provided four and set them in the middle of the table. She assumed it was to make her feel less self-conscious about being the only person at the table to order dessert. Not that she cared.

It was only a chocolate sundae. Caleb was about to sell his birthright.

She scooped up a mound of whipped cream.

"The house is on a separate well?" asked Nathan.

"A well for the house. One for the outbuildings, and a third for the staff quarters."

"Those cabins are all less than five years old," Frank put in. "They're a great draw for couples or families who are interested in working at the ranch."

"What about irrigation?" asked Nathan.

"Two-hundred acres are irrigated and seeded to hay," Caleb answered.

"Four-hundred," Mandy put in.

Everyone looked her way.

"They doubled it," she explained, seeing no reason to leave the man with a misconception.

"Thanks," said Caleb.

She waved her spoon in acknowledgment, then dug into the ice cream and warm fudge.

"There are water rights on the river." Frank produced a sheaf of papers. "Spelled out in the agreement with the state."

Mandy swallowed her smooth, cool mouthful. "You might want to tell him about the review."

Both Caleb's and Frank's eyes went wide. Nathan turned to look at her. "Review?"

"The water rights are up for review." She dug her spoon in again, going for a big glob of the thick, cooling fudge. "It's a provision under the regulations. The first stakeholders meeting is this weekend. Here. In Lyndon. You must have seen the notices."

"Well," Frank put in heartily. "I don't think it's so much a review of existing—"

Nathan's eyes narrowed across the table at Frank. "You knew about this?"

Mandy stopped midbite, taking in the men's expressions.

Nathan looked angry. Frank looked like a deer in the head-lights. While Caleb was glaring at her in obvious frustration.

Okay, can of worms, she'd own up to that. But surely they hadn't expected to keep the review a secret. The man deserved to know what he was getting into.

Nathan pushed back his chair and threw his napkin down on the table. "Thank you for your time, gentlemen. Ms. Jacobs."

Frank quickly hopped up. "It's not what you might think. If you'd like, I can email a link to the Colorado information site."

Nathan headed for the exit, with Frank hustling along behind.

Mandy finished the bite of fudge sauce.

"You did that on purpose," Caleb accused, as he waved a waiter over to the table.

"I did not." She brandished her spoon. "But I hope you're not going to sit there and defend a plan to keep Nathan Brooks in the dark about the water review."

"No one's officially served notice to the property owners."

"You *were* going to keep him in the dark," Mandy accused. She couldn't believe it. She never would have expected it of Caleb.

"And *you* were going to behave yourself at this meeting," he countered.

The waiter stopped beside their table.

"Glen Klavitt, on the rocks. A double," said Caleb.

"I can't believe you would intentionally keep a buyer in the dark."

"Hey, I'm not his nursemaid."

"But you know the water rights are under review."

"I also know it's a routine review. And we're talking about preliminary discussions to determine if there should even be an official review."

"You've been doing your homework." Despite her disap-pointment in his principles, Mandy had to admire that.

"Which is what Nathan Brooks ought to have done. And what he likely would have done, *after* he'd seen the ranch and maybe fallen in love with it. And at that point, he would have been far more interested in making a compromise and listening to reason."

Okay. Mandy had to admit, when you looked at it like that, Caleb wasn't completely amoral.

"You don't lead with your flaws, Mandy."

The waiter set Caleb's drink down on the table.

Caleb nodded his thanks. "Marketing 101."

"I never studied marketing," she told him, scooping up another bite of ice cream, feeling a little like celebrating now. The sale was dead. She had some more time to find Reed.

"Did you study manipulation?" Caleb asked.

"They didn't have it as an elective at Metro State."

"Too bad. You're a natural."

"Do you really think I did that on purpose?" She hadn't meant to scare Nathan off. Then again, her heart wasn't exactly on the side of selling, either.

"I think you were very effective."

She made a show of shaking her head. "You must have studied paranoia."

He took a swig of the scotch. "Are you trying to tell me, you had no idea telling him about the review might scare him off? None at all? It never occurred to you? Not for one second?"

Okay, so as the words were coming out of her mouth, particularly when she saw Caleb's expression, of course it had occurred to her. But it didn't seem prudent to admit that now. "I was simply providing information." She stuck to her original story.

"Serves me right," said Caleb, polishing off the drink. "I never should have brought you along."

Mandy battled a twinge of guilt, setting down her dessert spoon, deciding she'd had enough of the sweet concoction.

Frank returned to the table. "I'm afraid we lost him. Permanently." Then his affable expression hardened as he focused on Mandy. "And you. I trust you learned a valuable lesson—"

"Leave her out of it," Caleb immediately put in, tone dark.

"But—" Frank began. The he took in Caleb's expression and cut himself off.

"Win some, you lose some." Caleb tossed his credit card on the table. "Thank you for your time, Frank."

"I..." Frank snapped his mouth shut. "Right. I'll be in touch."

Caleb nodded a dismissal, and Frank deliberately straightened his suit jacket, tugged at the sleeves and headed for the exit.

"You didn't need to defend me," Mandy felt compelled to point out. Caleb standing up for her made her feel even guiltier than she had a few moments ago.

The waiter came by and smoothly accepted Caleb's credit card.

"It's none of his business what you do or do not say." Caleb swirled the ice cubes in his glass. "But it is my business. And it's my responsibility to make sure you're never in a position to do anything like that again."

The intensity of his expression made a shiver run through her. "That sounded like a threat."

He tapped his fingertips against the white tablecloth. "I don't threaten. It's a waste of time. I just deliver."

"In this instance—" she couldn't seem to stop herself from asking "—what exactly are you going to deliver?"

While she waited on his answer, he helped himself to one of the extra dessert spoons and took a scoop of the sundae. "You, Mandy Jacobs, are off the list."

Okay, that didn't sound too dire. "There's a list?"

He took his time savoring the mouthful of ice cream. "The list of people who are invited to my meetings with perspective buyers."

She took his lead and retrieved her own dessert spoon. "I thought I added value to the conversation. I was the one who knew about the four-hundred acres."

"I'll give you that," he allowed, scooping into a swirl of

whipped cream. "You were doing great, right up until you blew the entire deal."

"There's another way of looking at this, you know."

"And, how is that?"

"A second chance."

"Didn't you hear Frank? That buyer is gone for good."

She concentrated on mining a vein of the gooey fudge. "I didn't mean a second chance with the buyer. I meant, a chance to make the right decision."

"The right decision?"

"To change your mind about selling the ranch."

He rolled each of his shirtsleeves two folds up his forearms. "I can't wait to see how you try to sell this."

She licked her spoon, gathering her thoughts. "I don't think you can discount the possibility that this was fate."

"You telling Nathan Brooks he might not be able to water his cattle was fate?"

"Exactly."

"Please tell me that's not the end of your argument."

"First," she counted, "Nathan asks for a meeting with Frank. Second, you and I happen to be in Lyndon. Third, I happen to be free for dinner. And fourth, the subject of the water rights came up in conversation. Those are either four separate coincidences, or it's fate."

Caleb waggled his spoon. "Wow. You really had to reach for it, but that was a pretty good spin."

"Thank you." She took a bite.

"I'm not changing my mind."

"I'm only asking for a few more days, maybe a couple of weeks."

"I don't have a couple of weeks."

"Sure, you do. You've put this false sense of urgency on a situation that doesn't—"

"The Brazilian government is the one with the sense of urgency."

"I'll look after the ranch," she offered. "I can do it. You know I can. And then it'll be waiting when Reed—"

"Reed made his choice. And you have your own ranch to run."

"Travis's there to run—"

But Caleb was shaking his head. "Your family needs you, Mandy. And I'm not chasing after Reed like some preschool nanny. I've made my decision."

She set down her spoon, struggling to hold her temper, and struggling to stay calm. "Your decision is wrong."

He set aside his own spoon. "You might not like it, but it is the right thing to do. And there's nothing to be gained by prolonging it."

"Caleb—"

"No. I've listened. I've considered your perspective—"

"You're joking, right?"

The man hadn't considered anything. He was being closed-minded and reactionary. And he was going to destroy what was left of his family.

But Caleb's jaw went hard. "I've considered your perspective, Mandy. And I disagree. And that's that."

Now her temper was taking a firm hold. "And that's the end of the discussion?"

"That's the end of the discussion."

"I see." Mandy rose to her feet, and Caleb instantly followed suit.

She drew a sharp breath, looking him square in the eyes. "Then, thank you for dinner. I can find my own way back to the ranch."

"Is this your version of a temper tantrum?"

Mandy clamped her jaw tight.

"It's dark outside, Mandy. And it's starting to rain."

She didn't respond. She was an intelligent, capable, functioning adult. She didn't need a man to escort her home on a rainy night.

Before he could say anything else, she turned on her heel

and headed for the exit. At the very least, there were buses. She'd hop on a bus, and Travis or one of the hands could meet her at the end of the ranch road. They wouldn't mind.

"I'm getting us cottages at the Rose Inn," Caleb's deep voice came from behind her. "We'll drive back to the ranch tomorrow."

"Go away." He might be a sexy, intelligent, compelling man, but he was a stubborn jerk, and she didn't want anything more to do with him.

Mandy was still scowling when Caleb swung back into the driver's seat and handed her the key to cottage number six. He slammed the door shut behind him. The rain was now pounding down on the roof, and the wind was lashing the trees around them. Caleb's clothes and hair were soaked from the sprint to the small office building and back again.

"I'm in seven," he offered amicably. "We're down at the end of the river road." He pulled ahead, carefully maneuvering the SUV through the muddy ruts and around the deepest of the puddles.

"Thank you," she offered stiffly, eyes straight ahead.

"We should probably try to get away early in the morning," he continued, while the bright headlights bounced against the dripping, undulating aspen branches.

Mandy gripped the armrest and braced her feet against the floor.

"The restaurant opens at seven. That good for you?"

"I'll be ready," she said.

"Great." He supposed he'd have to be content with her agreeing to drive with him at all. Cordiality was probably still a fair way down the road.

The dark outline of a two-story cottage came into view. His headlights picked up the signs for numbers six and seven on the post out front. There were porches on both stories and a long staircase running between them.

"You're on top," he told Mandy as he brought the vehicle as close to the building as possible.

She reached for the car door handle.

"Hang on," he cautioned, opening his own door.

He quickly rounded the hood as she opened her door. His boots sank into the mud, and a river of water flowed over them.

"Hold still," he told her, putting a hand out to stop her progress. He reached into the vehicle to lift her from the seat.

"Back off," she warned him, holding up a finger.

"Don't be ridiculous." Undeterred, he slid an arm around the small of her back. "There's no sense in both of us ruining our shoes."

"I've waded through mud before."

"Bully for you." He wove his other arm beneath her jean-covered knees. "Hang on."

"This is ridiculous," she muttered, but her arms went around his neck, anchoring her to him.

He straightened and shoved the door shut with his knee. Then he ducked his head over hers and mounted the stairs.

"Key?" he asked, setting her down as they made it to the narrow shelter in front of the cottage door.

"Right here." With dripping hands, she inserted the key into the lock.

Caleb turned the door handle, yawing the door wide into the dark room. He felt for the light switch on the inside wall, finding it, flipping it, bringing two lamps to life on either side of the king-size bed.

The room was peak-ceilinged and airy, with a cream-colored love seat and two padded armchairs at the far end. The living room grouping bracketed a sliding-glass door that opened to a small balcony. The bed was covered in an English country floral quilt, with six plump pillows and a gauzy canopy. Candles and knickknacks lined the mantel above a false fireplace. And a small kitchenette next to the bathroom door completed the suite.

"They said the heater was tricky," Caleb explained to

Mandy, crouching down next to the propane unit, squinting at the faded writing on the knobs.

"I'm not cold," she told him.

He pressed the red button, turning the black knob to pilot. "If you do get cold, you can adjust it up like this." He turned to find her still standing next to the open door. "Will you come and look?"

"I'm sure it's not that complicated."

"You're behaving like a two-year-old."

"Because I won't roll over and play dead? I have to wonder what kind of people you employ, Caleb. Do you have a string of yes-men who follow you around all day, never questioning your infinite wisdom?"

"No," he answered simply, deciding he liked it better when she was giving him the silent treatment. "Do you want to know how to work the heater or not?"

"Not."

He shrugged and rose to his feet, dusting off his hands. "Suit yourself."

Refusing to cater to her temper any longer, he crossed the room, bid her good night and firmly closed the door behind him, trotting swiftly down the staircase to open his own cottage.

His suite was slightly larger than Mandy's, but with the same English country look, deep mattress, plump pillows and floral curtains. He adjusted his own heater, slipped off his wet leather boots and stripped his way out of his soaking clothes.

The cottage provided a health kit with a toothbrush, toothpaste, comb, shaving razor and cream, along with a few other necessities, including scented body wash, which he set aside in favor of the plain bar of soap.

Half an hour later, Caleb felt refreshed. He'd opened the minibar to find a light beer, chose a magazine from the selection on the coffee table and stretched out under the quilt in his boxers.

He entered the password into his phone and chose the email

icon. He scrolled through the messages, finding one from Danielle labeled *stranded*. With an anticipatory grin, he clicked it open, scanning his way through a series of complaints, threats and colorful swearwords.

He responded, telling her he'd be back to the ranch tomorrow morning with a box full of auto parts and a fat, bonus check. He didn't let on that Travis had told him the whole story. He might as well let Danielle keep some of her dignity.

He dealt with the most pressing issues on his phone, then switched to the sports magazine, finding an article on his favorite basketball team. He read it and then checked the NASCAR stats. A crack of thunder rumbled in the distance, and the wind picked up outside. Sudden waves of rain battered the windowpanes, while the lights flickered, putting the room in darkness for a split second.

A few power flickers later, Caleb felt himself dozing off, and he set the magazine aside.

The next thing he knew, he was jolted awake by a deafening crash. The room was in pitch darkness, and the storm howled on outside. He rocketed out of bed, rushing to the window, guessing at the direction of the sound.

A flash of lightning revealed the Escalade was intact. But a large tree had fallen across the dirt road, crushing the low fence in front of the cottage, its topmost branches resting against the front wall. Perfect. They were going to need a chain saw before they could go anywhere in the morning.

He let the curtain drop, and as he did, a loud, long crack reverberated through the building. Before he could react, a roar shattered the air and the building jolted, wood groaning and splintering in the night.

Caleb was out the door in a shot, taking the stairs three at a time, terrified that the tree had come through the roof and Mandy had been hurt. He flung open her door. It was either unlocked or he'd broken it down. He wasn't sure which. But his entire body shuddered in relief at the sight of her standing

next to the sofa, peering out the glass doors, lightning illumi-
nating the room like a strobe light.

"It was a tree," she told him, turning in her bra and panties.
"Sheared the balcony railing right off."

He strode across the room. "Are you okay?"

She nodded. "I'm fine. Wow. That's some storm going on
out there." Lightning strikes were coming one after the other,
thunder following almost instantaneously.

"I don't think you're safe up here." He found himself putting
a protective arm around her shoulders. His gaze went reflexively to her sky-blue bra and silky underwear. It was completely inappropriate to stare, but he couldn't help himself.

"I'm fine," she argued. "How many trees can possibly—"

Another tree cracked and crashed in the woods nearby.

She blinked at him. "This must be the storm of the century."

"Put your clothes on," he told her. There was no way he was
leaving her up here.

She glanced down at her body, seeming to suddenly remember what she was wearing. She quickly folded her arms across
her breasts.

"I'm not looking," he lied. "Now, let's get downstairs." He
wanted a sturdy story between them and any falling debris.

Mandy crossed the room and struggled into her jeans, slipping her arms into her shirtsleeves.

Caleb tried mightily not to watch, but he couldn't stop himself from taking a few surreptitious glances.

"Should we call the office?" she asked.

"I think they've long since closed. And I'm pretty sure they
know the property's getting wind damage. Nobody should go
out in this."

"I guess staying here is the safest," she agreed, tucking her
messy hair behind her ears as she bent to put on her boots.

She turned then, and she seemed to realize for the first time
that he was nearly naked.

"I rushed up here," he defended. "I thought you might be
hurt."

Her mouth tightened into a smirk. "You're a knight in shining...boxers?"

He crossed to the door and pulled it open. "You can't embarrass me."

She moved toward him. "Not modest?"

"Not at all. You can see me naked any old time you want."

"Pass," she tossed over her shoulder, striding out into the rain.

He shut the door tight, double-checking it before he followed her downstairs. Rain splattered against his hair, wind chilling his wet skin, while the lightning and thunder continued to crack through the black sky.

In his own suite, he lit a couple of the decorative candles, dried off with a towel and switched his wet boxers for his damp jeans. Going commando under his jeans wasn't the most comfortable feeling in the world, but his options were limited.

She stood in the middle of the room, hands on her hips. "I suppose you'll want the bed."

He flipped back the comforter and stretched out. The love seat would barely fit a ten-year-old. "You're welcome to share," he told her.

"I don't think that's a good idea."

"As opposed to one of us staying awake all night? It's a big bed, Mandy."

"Can I trust you?"

He rolled his eyes. "Trust me to do what? Not to attack you while you sleep?" He leaned over and pulled back the opposite edge of the covers. "Give me a break, Mandy."

The thunder rumbled as she took a single, hesitant step forward, looking decidedly uncertain. Not that he blamed her. Despite his bold words, it was going to be a challenge to keep his hands to himself.

"Can I trust *you?*" he countered, hoping to keep things light.

"Ha. I'm still mad at you."

"Doesn't mean I'm not hot," he goaded.

In response, she marched defiantly to the bed. "You're not that hot."

"I'm sorry to hear that."

She stuck her nose in the air, turned her back and plunked down on the edge of the bed, tugging off her boots and dropping them to the wooden floor. Her socks followed. Then her hand went to the snap of her jeans, and he heard the zipper pull down, and she shimmied out of them.

Okay, he was a gentleman, and he was proud of his self-control. But, good grief. Was the woman insane?

Six

An insistent, intermittent buzzing dragged Mandy from the depths of a deep sleep. She was comfortable, toasty warm, and she sincerely hoped it wasn't time to get up yet.

As consciousness returned, she felt Caleb shift against her. She knew she should recoil in shock at having cuddled up to him while she slept. But his big body felt so good against her own, that she decided to pretend she was asleep for a few more seconds.

The buzzing stopped, and his deep, husky voice penetrated the darkness. "Yeah?"

He didn't pull away, either, and she let herself sink into the forbidden sensations. She'd kept her blouse on, while he was wearing his blue jeans, so there was no danger of intimate skin contact. Still, her belly was snuggled up to his hip, her breast against his arm and her calf against his.

"Anybody hurt?" His voice sounded stronger, and her brain engaged more thoroughly on his words. "Good. So, how bad is it?"

She heard the rustle as he swiped a hand across his forehead, into his hairline, and she could picture him blinking his eyes open in the darkness.

"Tell her to call Orson Mallek. He can source the parts worldwide." Caleb shifted, his arm grazing her nipple, and it was all she could do not to gasp in reaction. "A week will cripple us," he said. "Tell them forty-eight hours max."

Arousal invaded her system, hijacking reason. The urge to wrap herself around Caleb and give in to her desires, to hell with the consequences, was quickly gaining traction in her brain.

"Colorado," he said into the phone.

She felt him shift, and knew he was squinting at her in the dim light, probably wondering if she was awake or asleep. It was getting to the point of unreasonable that she could have slept through the conversation.

It was time to put up or shut up.

Grabbing a final scarp of sanity, she drew away, shifting onto her back, putting some space between them.

"Call me when you know something. Thanks."

"Something wrong?" she asked sleepily, hoping against hope he'd buy that she'd only just woken up.

"A breakdown in the chassis plant."

"Is it serious?"

"Depends on how long it takes to repair." He moved to his side, propping on an elbow, facing her in the predawn glow. "We can go a couple of days before we have to start cutting back shifts. After a week, we're looking at temporary layoffs. I hate to have to do that."

She found herself curious. "How many people work for your company?"

"In that plant, a few hundred."

"Overall?"

"I don't know. Thousands, anyway."

"You have thousands of people working for you?" It defied Mandy's imagination.

"Not directly." He chuckled.

"Nobody works for me."

"And you don't work for anyone else, either. It's a whole lot simpler that way."

"Technically, I work for my dad. Though," she allowed, "that's definitely going to change for a while."

"Who'll take over the ranch?" Caleb asked, laying his head back down on the pillow. "Is Seth the heir apparent?"

Mandy thought about it. "It's hard to say. Especially with his mayor campaign coming up. Travis's the most hands-on of us all, but he's more of a day to day, roll up his sleeves guy. Seth definitely takes the strategic view, but he's not out on the range very often these days. Abigail's the organized one. She knows pretty much everything about everything."

"And you?" Caleb asked. "What's your strength?"

"I don't know. Diplomacy, maybe."

He chuckled. "You have got to be kidding me."

"Hey," she protested. "People like me. I broker compromises all the time."

"Not for me, you didn't."

"Jury's still out on that one. I predict that someday you'll be thanking me for my role last night."

"I wouldn't hold your breath."

"My point is—" she fought the urge to engage further in a debate with him about selling the ranch "—we all have different strengths."

"What about your other sister, the little one?"

"Katrina?"

"I haven't seen her yet."

Mandy resettled herself, bending one knee, which brushed up against Caleb's thigh. She let it rest there, pretending she didn't realize she was touching him. "That's right. You left before it happened."

"What happened?" There was concern in his voice.

"Nothing bad," Mandy hastily put in. "Katrina attended a fine arts boarding school in New York City. She's still in New York. A principle dancer with Liberty Ballet Company."

"Seriously?"

"I'm serious. She loves it. Then again, she always did hate the ranch."

His tone turned contemplative. "So, Lyndon Valley produced more than one city dweller."

"You two would probably have a lot in common." Mandy kept her voice flip, careful not to betray her disquiet at the thought of Caleb and Katrina. She wasn't jealous of her baby sister. She'd never cared about being glamorous before, and she wasn't about to start now.

"What about you?" Caleb asked. "Do you like the ranch, living and working so closely with your family?"

"Absolutely." Mandy couldn't imagine any other life. She loved the quiet, the simplicity, the slower pace and the wide-open spaces.

"What about when you get married?"

"Nobody's asked me yet."

"You plan to raise your children on the ranch?"

"I do." She nodded with conviction. "Kids need fresh air, hard work, a sense of responsibility and purpose."

Caleb was silent for a long moment.

"What about you?" Mandy asked. "You plan to raise your children in a high-rise apartment?"

He stretched onto his back, lacing his fingers behind his head. "That's a very long way off."

"But you do plan to have children one day."

"I don't know." He sighed. "I didn't have much of a role model for a father."

"You're nothing like he was."

"I'm nothing like your father, either." He turned to look at her. "He's a fantastic family man. I'm better at business, focused, driven and narcissistic."

"You cared that you might have to lay people off just now," she pointed out. "That isn't narcissistic behavior. It is empathetic, compassionate behavior."

He turned toward her again, his thigh coming fully up

against hers, his midnight-blue gaze capturing hers in the gathering dawn. "You comfortable behind those rose-colored glasses?"

"You cared, Caleb."

"I'm not the devil incarnate. But that doesn't mean I should be raising children."

"What *do* you want to do? With your future?"

"I've been thinking in two- or three-month increments for an awful long time now."

"Okay," she allowed. "Where do you want to be in three months?"

His gaze softened on hers, and he reached out to smooth back a lock of her hair. "I can tell you where I want to be in five minutes."

Her chest hitched, and her lungs tightened around an indrawn breath. His finger traced down the curve of her cheek, along her neck, to trace the vee of her blouse. Her pulse jumped and prickly heat formed on her skin.

"You took off your jeans," he told her in a husky voice. "Why did you take off your jeans?"

"They're uncomfortable to sleep in."

"I thought it was to make me crazy."

She shook her head. "You kept your pants on, I figured we were safe enough."

His mouth curved in a small smile. "Since you cuddle in your sleep?"

"I never knew I did that." She felt as though she could fall forever into the depths of his sexy eyes. "I've never slept with a man before."

"No way."

"I was in a girls dorm in college."

His hand dropped away, and his expression turned guarded. "You're not..."

"A virgin?" She couldn't help but laugh at the guilt on his face. "Didn't I just tell you I went to college?"

"You scare me, Mandy."

She sobered, unfamiliar feelings bubbling to life inside her. She might not be a virgin, but her experience was with swaggering eighteen- and nineteen-year-olds. They were about as different from Caleb as a person could get.

"You scare me, too," she told him on a whisper.

"Scaring you is the last thing I want to do."

She nodded, and he slowly leaned in to kiss her.

His lips were firm but soft, confident as they slanted across hers. They parted, hot and delicious. And he pressed her back into the pillow, one arm snaking around the small of her back, pulling her up against him.

A surge of desire swelled inside her. Her back instinctively arched, and she parted her own lips, opening to his tongue, savoring the intense flavor of his passion. Her arms went around his neck, anchoring her, while her breasts rubbed against his chest. Her nipples went hard, tight, intensely sensitive.

He groaned, sliding his hand down her hip, over her silky panties, down her bare thigh. His kisses wandered along the crook of her neck, circling her ear, separating her blouse to kiss his way to the tip of her shoulder.

She pressed her lips against his neck, drawing his skin into the heat of her mouth, tasting salt and dried rainwater. His hand convulsed on her bottom, voice going hoarse. "You're killing me, Mandy."

"Is that good?" It felt good from her side. Very, very good.

He kissed her shoulder, kissed her neck, kissed her mouth, dragging her pelvis tight against his. "You need to tell me yes or no."

She opened her mouth to say yes.

But he pulled back, and his sober expression stopped her.

"I…" She suddenly hesitated. This wasn't college. This was far more complicated than college.

"We step over this cliff," he warned her in an undertone, "we can't come back again."

She struggled to interpret his words. "Are you saying no?" she asked in a small voice.

When he didn't answer, her stomach clenched tight. Was she being swept along on this tidal wave alone? How humiliating. She stiffened.

When he finally answered, his voice was controlled and compassionate. "I'm saying you're not the kind of woman I usually date. You need to think about this."

She pulled back farther, feeling as if she'd been doused in cold water. She hardened her tone. "Excellent suggestion."

Without giving him a chance to say anything more, she flounced out of the bed and snagged her jeans from the floor. "In fact, now that you mention it, breakfast is probably a much better idea."

She strode her way toward the bathroom, hoping against hope the light was too dim for him to get a good view of her scantily clad rear end.

Feet apart, wearing the brand-new pair of steel-toed boots he'd purchased at the Lyndon shopping mall, Caleb chainsawed his way through the third fallen tree on Bainbridge Avenue. The physical work felt good, and tearing trees apart gave him an outlet for his sexual frustration.

Lyndon was a mess this morning. Mandy hadn't been far off when she'd guessed last night was the storm of the century. The wind, rain—and even hail in some places—had taken down trees, damaged buildings and sent several people to the hospital. Fortunately, no one had serious injuries.

Mandy was on the clearing crew a few hundred yards down the road. Hands protected by leather gloves, with about a dozen other people, she was hauling branches and sections of tree trunk to waiting pickup trucks. Though Caleb's gaze strayed to her over and over again, he told himself that this morning had been for the best. If she wasn't ready, she wasn't ready. And he wasn't going to push her into something she'd regret.

In other parts of town, Caleb knew many other crews were working, while construction experts, carpenters and engineers assessed the damage to buildings and other town infrastructure.

His phone buzzed in his breast pocket, and he shut down the chain saw, setting it on the ground by his feet. He stripped off his leather gloves, releasing the pocket button and fumbling his way into the deep pocket to address the persistent buzzing.

"Terrell here," he barked shortly.

"Caleb? It's Seth."

"Oh, hey, Seth." Caleb swiped back his sweaty hair. "Everything all right with your dad?"

"Better and better. They're going to start some physical and speech therapies in a few days."

"That's great news."

"Agreed. Listen, have you seen any of the storm coverage? It's all about how bad Lyndon got hit last night."

"We're in the thick of it," Caleb replied, glancing around once more at the destruction. "Mandy and I are still in town."

Seth's tone turned worried. "Is she okay?"

"She's a hundred percent. We're helping out with the cleanup."

"Good. That's a relief. Listen, the cleanup is what I wanted to talk to you about. As the president of Active Equipment, is there a possibility of you making a donation to the town? Maybe a couple of loaders."

"Absolutely," Caleb responded, wondering why he hadn't thought of it himself. "Let me see which dealers are closest, and how quickly they can respond."

"That would be terrific."

"Hey, no problem. They can use all the help they can get here."

"And…uh…Caleb?"

"Yeah?"

"Would you be comfortable with me making the public announcement? I don't want to steal your PR or anything."

Caleb got it. "But it wouldn't hurt your mayoralty campaign any to be the front man on this?"

"Exactly."

"Hey, go for it," said Caleb. "It was your idea. You deserve the credit."

"Thanks." Seth's tone was heartfelt.

"Happy to help out. Are you coming into town?"

"I'm going to try. But it may take a while. The airport's closed."

"Wow." Caleb was surprised to learn about the airport. "I'm working on Bainbridge. This thing must have hit the entire town."

"Get to a television when you can. They've got aerials."

"I'm on the business end of a chain saw for the moment. And I think power's out all over the place."

"Mandy's okay?" Seth confirmed.

"She's a trouper," said Caleb, his gaze going to where she struggled with a section of tree trunk that had to be thirty-six inches across. To his astonishment, she smiled while she worked, obviously making a joke to the man beside her.

"That, she is," Seth agreed. "I'll be there as soon as I can."

"Roger, that." Caleb signed off.

After making a few calls to Active Equipment headquarters and giving them Seth's contact information, Caleb resettled his gloves and yanked on the pull cord for the chain saw. The action restarted the engine, and he braced his foot on the big log in front of him, ripping his way through the next section of the downed cedar tree.

Working methodically, he made it to the end of the tree, sheering off branches and bucking the trunk into manageable sections. Then he glanced up to see Travis approaching, thirty feet away.

Caleb shut it down again, wiping his forehead. "Where'd you come from?"

Travis glanced around. "Whoa. This is unbelievable."

"Tell me about it. You should have heard them coming down last night. You here to help?"

"I am now." He tugged a pair of work gloves out of the back pocket of his jeans. "My original plan was to bring Danielle in to the airport."

Caleb glanced around but didn't see Danielle among the workers. "Airport's closed."

"We know that now. But she was getting pretty antsy this morning."

"Where is she?"

"I dropped her off at the coffee bar. She wasn't exactly dressed for brush clearing."

Caleb cracked a smile. "I think it would be dangerous to let her loose out here."

"She might break a nail?"

"She might get somebody killed."

Travis raked a hand through his short hair. "Yeah, she's definitely better with a computer than with power tools. She's making calls to see what her options are for getting back to Chicago."

"She can take my jet," Caleb offered, seeing an opportunity to make amends for some of the unfortunate complications of her trip to Colorado.

Caleb retrieved his phone and dialed Danielle's cell. He made the offer of the jet and asked her to touch base with Seth to make sure the heavy-equipment donation went quickly and smoothly. Then he signed off.

"That'll give her something productive to do," he told Travis.

Travis glanced around. "Where do you need me?"

"See the tall kid in the blue T-shirt?"

"At the black pickup?"

"He's keeping the chain saws fueled and sharp. Grab one, and you can start at the other end of that tree." Caleb pointed as he moved on. "If we can open up this next hundred yards, we'll have a corridor to the highway."

"Will do," said Travis. "By the way, it was nice of you to let Seth organize that equipment donation."

"His idea," said Caleb, flipping the switch and setting up to restart the chain saw. "Besides, Lyndon will be lucky to have him as mayor."

Mandy hopped up onto the tailgate of a pickup truck to take a break from the heavy hauling work. She was tired and sweating, and her shoulders were getting sore.

Somebody put a cup of coffee in her hand. She offered her thanks and took a grateful sip. She normally took cream and sugar, but she wasn't about to complain. It was nearly two in the afternoon, and she'd been hauling brush steadily since breakfast.

Her animosity toward Caleb had been forgotten when the sun came up and they saw what the storm had done. In fact, it seemed frivolous now to have even been thinking about love-making this morning.

"You eaten anything?" Danielle's voice startled Mandy, and she glanced up to see the perfectly pressed woman picking her way across the debris-strewn road to the pickup truck.

"What are you doing here?" Mandy couldn't help exclaiming.

Danielle was wearing slacks today, but they looked like expensive, dove-gray linen, and they were topped with a jewel-encrusted mauve sweater and paired with pewter-colored calfskin boots. Her makeup was perfect, and not a single hair was out of place.

"Travis brought me into town."

"Travis's here?" Mandy glanced around, but didn't catch a glimpse of her brother.

"I was hoping to catch a flight to Chicago. But the airport's closed."

As Danielle arrived at the truck, Mandy looked for a blanket or a stray piece of clothing to throw on the tailgate to protect the woman's expensive slacks. She spotted a quilted shirt, grabbed it and shook it out, laying it inside up on the tailgate and motioning to it.

"Thank you," said Danielle, awkwardly hopping up and settling herself. She snapped open her designer handbag and extracted a deli sandwich, handing it to Mandy.

"You're a saint." Mandy sighed, accepting the offer.

"You're amazing," Danielle returned. "How on earth can you work this hard?"

"Practice." Mandy took a big bite of the thick sandwich.

"Well." Danielle smoothed her slacks, setting her handbag down in her lap. She gave a delicate, self-deprecating laugh. "I've been dialing my fingers to the bone."

Mandy smiled at the joke. "Nobody expects you to do manual labor. Anymore than they'd expect me to compose a legal brief."

"That's very kind of you to say."

"Don't even worry about it. Thanks for the sandwich."

They sat in silence for a moment, the sound of chain saws, truck engines and shouts surrounding them. Bainbridge Street was a hive of activity.

"I've been working with your brother Seth."

Mandy swallowed. "On what?"

"Caleb's having him coordinate a donation from Active Equipment to the town of Lyndon, loaders, backhoes, etc. He'll be on Channel Ten to make the announcement in a few minutes."

Mandy's tone went thoughtful. "Really?" Her gaze went to where Caleb was bucking up trees. "I assume it's a political stunt?"

"Move," said Danielle. "A political move. And a smart one. Everybody wins."

"I suppose they do." Though it seemed a little slick to Mandy, she couldn't say she saw any serious flaws.

"Speaking of everybody wins…" Danielle looked straight at Mandy. "I have an idea."

"For Seth's campaign?" Mandy hoped it didn't involve her. She was planning to stay firmly on the ranch and out of sight throughout the mayor race.

"For finding Reed."

Mandy swallowed, her attention perking up. "I'm listening."

"I don't know how long it normally takes to sell a thirty-million-dollar ranch. But, I'm assuming it's a while." She brushed some imaginary lint from the front of her slacks. "So, I've been thinking, and I've come to the conclusion that my best interests may be the same as your best interests."

Her gaze drifted to Caleb. "He's having a little too much fun out here. I need him back on the job, and the shortest route to that end would appear to be finding Reed."

"You think he's having fun?" Mandy couldn't help interjecting. "He hates it here. He can't wait to leave."

"So he says."

"He doesn't want to be in Colorado," Mandy insisted. And he sure didn't want to be in the Lyndon Valley, on his own ranch, surrounded by painful memories.

Danielle smiled patiently, and a wealth of wisdom seemed to simmer in her dark brown eyes. "I'm not going to take that chance." Then she became all business. "Here's what we're going to do. You're going to give me your cell phone, and I'm going to dial a number, and you're going to talk to a man named Enrico. Tell him everything you know about Reed's disappearance."

Mandy hesitated. She couldn't help remembering Danielle's suggestion that they track Reed's credit-card use. She wanted to find him, but this felt a little too off the beaten path for her. "Is Enrico a code name?"

Danielle's laughter tinkled. "His name is Enrico Rossi. He's a private investigator."

"Would I be breaking the law?"

"You? No?"

Mandy felt her eyes go wide, and her blood pressure slipped up a notch. "But Enrico will?"

Danielle cocked her head. "I haven't the first clue what Enrico might or might not do. But he will find Reed."

Mandy was tempted. Frightened, but tempted. "Will I go to jail for this?"

"None of his clients have so far."

Mandy tried to figure out if Danielle was joking. "You're scary, you know that?"

"I'm practical." Danielle waved a dismissive hand. "There's an off chance he'll hack a password or two, but he's not going to steal anything, and he's certainly not going to harm anyone. And, since you won't be paying him, there's absolutely no legal trail that leads back to you."

"I won't be paying him?" This was sounding stranger and stranger all the time.

"He owes me a favor."

Mandy felt her shoulder slump. "Good grief."

"It's nothing clandestine or mysterious. I was his defense attorney. Pro bono. When I was first out of law school."

"So, he's a criminal." A criminal who could find Reed and stop Caleb from making a colossal mistake that would reverberate for generations. Where was the moral balance on that?

"He had a misspent youth."

"What did he do?" Mandy was absolutely not getting caught up with thieves and murderers, not even to find Reed.

"He was a big bad street kid, who got into a fight with another big bad street kid, who it turned out, was trying to recruit Enrico's little brother into a gang. Enrico won. He was charged with assault. I got him off."

That didn't sound so bad. In fact, it sounded kind of noble. "What happened to his brother?"

"He just won a scholarship to UIC. He wants to go into law."

"So, Enrico's a good guy?"

"Enrico's a great guy. Eat your sandwich, and we'll make the call."

It turned out that Enrico didn't sound remotely like a tough, streetwise criminal. He was articulate and seemed intelligent, and he said he was confident he would find Reed. When

Mandy saw Caleb and Travis approaching the pickup truck, she quickly finished the call and disconnected.

"Thanks," she whispered to Danielle as the two men approached.

"You look unexpectedly cheerful," Travis said to Danielle.

While Caleb focused on Mandy. "You holding up okay?"

"I'm feeling optimistic," Danielle responded, sending a brief glance to Mandy.

"I'm just fine," Mandy answered Caleb. She drew a breath, both nervous and excited after her call with Enrico.

"Pretty hard work," Caleb observed.

"Piece of cake," Mandy responded with a shrug. She was tired, and she'd definitely be sore in the morning, but she still had a good few hours left in her.

Danielle retrieved two more sandwiches from her purse and passed them to the men. Both smiled and voiced their thanks, digging right in.

"Any news from the outside world?" Caleb asked Danielle between bites.

"Seth should have made the announcement on air by now. Equipment will be on a flatbed truck coming out of Northridge this afternoon. They're hoping to have the airport up and running by tomorrow. And I was able to book a couple of rooms at the Sunburst Hotel." She looked to Travis. "I guessed you might want to stay over?"

"You guessed right," he responded, glancing around at the destruction. "They'll need me another day at least."

"Mandy and I can keep our cottages at the Rose," Caleb put in. "Apparently, they're structurally sound. Though they can't guarantee we'll have electricity. But they did offer us a discount."

"I'll take the cottage at the Rose," Travis put in. "Mandy can stay at the Sunburst with Danielle. She'll be more comfortable there."

Caleb's jaw tightened, and his eyes narrowed in what was obvious annoyance at Travis's unilateral decree.

"Sure," Mandy quickly agreed. She didn't care where she slept. It wasn't as if she and Caleb had plans for a clandestine meeting.

She might have been swept off her feet in his bed this morning. But she'd had plenty of time to reframe her mind-set. Caleb had been right to suggest some sober second thought on the matter. Making love with him would have been a colossal mistake. One she had no intention of making.

Seven

All the way back from Lyndon, Caleb told himself he had done the right thing by giving Mandy the option to change her mind. It was the honorable thing to do, and he didn't regret it for one minute. Though he'd desired her beyond reason, he couldn't ignore the fact that she wasn't worldly, she was a family friend, and compared to the women he normally dated, she was quite innocent—in a fresh, compelling way that even now had him wishing he could have thrown caution to the wind.

Damn it.

He had to get her out of his head.

He pushed the door to the Terrell ranch house open, forcing himself to walk into the quiet gloom. Without Mandy or Danielle here, the place seemed to echo around him. He dropped the small duffel bag he'd bought in Lyndon onto the floor of the hall, flipped on a light and made his way into the living room.

Ghosts of his memories hovered in every room, in every knickknack, in every piece of furniture. He'd liked it in Lyndon. It had been a long time since he'd worked that hard physically, longer still since he'd had that sense of community and accomplishment.

He wondered what was going on at the Jacobses' place. He pictured Mandy, imagined her voice, her laughter, her jokes and the convoluted rationale for her contrary opinions. He missed her arguments most of all.

The vision disappeared, and the silence of the house closed in around him. A small, family portrait propped up on the mantel, seemed to mock his presence.

He moved closer, squinting at it.

The picture had been taken when Caleb and Reed were about fifteen. His father had dressed them up, gathered them together in the living room and insisted on wide, happy-looking smiles. Seeing it now, all Caleb could remember was that his father had screamed at Reed earlier that day, pushing him to the ground and demanding he resand an entire section of fence because of some perceived flaw.

He lifted the photo. If he looked closely, he could see that Reed's hands had been bleeding. Closer, still, and he could see his and Reed's brittle eyes. His mother had the haunted look that Caleb remembered so vividly. Though he'd pushed the memories away after he'd left, the fear that he hadn't known the half of his mother's anguish rushed back now.

If he'd known back then what he knew now, he'd might have taken a shotgun to his father. He should have taken a shotgun to his father. He'd have spent the rest of his life in jail, but his mother would have lived, and his brother would have been spared ten years of hell.

He glared at his father's expression, the false smile, the ham fists, the mouth that had spewed abuse, sending fear into the hearts of everyone around him.

Caleb's hand tightened on the frame.

Before the impulse turned into a conscious thought, he reflexively smashed the picture into the stone hearth. Glass shattered in all directions, the wooden frame splintered into three pieces, mangling the photo. He gripped the mantel with

FREE Merchandise is 'in the Cards' for you!

Dear Reader,

We're giving away FREE MERCHANDISE!

Seriously, we'd like to reward you for reading this novel by giving you **FREE MERCHANDISE** worth over $20. And no purchase is necessary!

You see the Jack of Hearts sticker above? Paste that sticker in the box on the Free Merchandise Voucher inside. Return the Voucher promptly...and we'll send you valuable Free Merchandise!

Thanks again for reading one of our novels—and enjoy your Free Merchandise with our compliments!

Pam Powers

Pam Powers

P.S. Look inside to see what Free Merchandise is **"in the cards"** for you!

H-D-01/12

The Reader Service - Here's how it works:

BUSINESS REPLY MAIL
FIRST-CLASS MAIL   PERMIT NO. 717   BUFFALO, NY

POSTAGE WILL BE PAID BY ADDRESSEE

THE READER SERVICE
PO BOX 1867
BUFFALO NY 14240-9952

NO POSTAGE
NECESSARY
IF MAILED
IN THE
UNITED STATES

both hands, closing his eyes, concentrating on obliterating the memories.

"And you really think selling the place will bring you closure?" Mandy's voice was soft but implacable from the entryway.

Caleb straightened and squared his shoulders. "I didn't hear you come in."

"No kidding."

"I need a shower." He turned on his heel, heading for the staircase, stripping off his shirt as he crossed the room. He wasn't fit company right now. And he wasn't going to let himself take his temper out on Mandy. What he needed was to scald some of his anger away.

Hopefully, when he finished, she'd have the sense to be gone.

He hit the top of the stairs, and pivoted around the corner, tossing his shirt to the ground and reaching for the snap of his jeans. He passed his brother's room; a shiver ran up his spine. His feet came to a halt, and he stood still for a long moment, gritting his teeth, his fists clenched, a sharp pain pounding through the center of his forehead. He swallowed hard, then kept walking, slamming the bathroom door behind him.

He twisted the taps full on and finished stripping off his grimy clothes. Then he wrestled the shower curtain out of the way and stepped into the deep tub. Under the pulsing spray, he scrubbed his body, shampooed his hair, then he stood there, staring at the familiar tile pattern until the water finally turned cold.

He turned the taps to Off, and the nozzle dripped to a stop while he valiantly tried to stuff his memories back into their box. He was beginning to realize he never should have come here.

There was a tentative rap on the bathroom door. "Caleb? You okay?"

He flung the curtain aside in frustration. "Go home, Mandy."

There was silence on the other side.

"I mean it," he shouted. The gentleman in him was exhausted, and he didn't have the fight left to keep his hands off her. She needed to get far away.

"Right," came a short, angry response. It was followed by a few footfalls and then silence.

Thank goodness.

He methodically toweled off, then rubbed a circle in the steam of the mirror. Once again, he borrowed his brother's shaving gear, telling himself that getting cleaned up, eating a decent meal and getting a good night's sleep would give him some perspective. The memories were from ten years ago, not from yesterday. It would be easier to get rid of them this time.

Finished shaving, he wiped his face and tossed the towel into the hamper in the corner of the bathroom. Naked, he turned and opened the door, and found Mandy sitting cross-legged on the floor across the hall.

He barked out a pithy swearword, while she quickly turned her head, squeezing her eyes shut.

"What the hell are you doing?" he demanded.

"I didn't want to leave," she squeaked, coming to her feet, face turned to the side, eyes still squeezed shut. "You seemed really upset downstairs."

"And you couldn't have foreseen *this?*" He wrapped a towel tightly around his waist, stuffing in the loose end.

"At our house, we don't… I mean, there are six of us living there."

"Well, there's nobody else living here." There was no need for him to cover up to cross the hall.

"Sorry."

Her contrite voice took the fight right out of him. It wasn't her fault. What the hell was the matter with him, anyway?

"Don't worry about it." Truth be told, he was more sorry about giving her an eyeful than he was about being seen naked. He couldn't care less about that.

"I'm the one who's sorry," he offered.

She opened one eye and cautiously peeked back at him.

He propped his bare shoulder against the doorjamb and folded his arms over his chest. "What are you doing here, Mandy?"

"We haven't had a chance to talk. You know, alone. Since…"

"Since you turned me down that morning in Lyndon?" It had been the topmost thing on his mind, too.

Her brows went up. "You mean, since *you* turned *me* down."

That sure as hell wasn't the way he remembered it. "You were the one who said you preferred breakfast."

"You were the one who said I should think about it."

"So?"

Her voice rose. "So, who tells a girl who's kissing him back to *think about it?*"

"Someone who's a gentleman and not a frat boy."

"I thought you'd changed your mind."

"I thought you'd changed yours."

She took a step toward him. "So, what you meant was…"

He straightened away from the doorjamb and met her in the middle of the hall, letting his desire for her pulse free once more. "What I meant was that you needed to be sure."

"I'm definitely not sure," she admitted.

"That's what I thought." He swallowed his disappointment, and he told himself he had no right to be annoyed.

In the silence that followed, she lifted her index finger and pushed it tentatively toward his bare chest. Before she could touch him, he snagged her wrist and held it fast. His gaze bore into hers. "I'm not going to let you do this to me again." He was a man, not a saint. And she'd have to practice her little seduction games somewhere else.

She took a step in, brushing up against him, her eyes going smoky, her lips slightly parted in an invitation that was clear as day. "So, your answer is no?"

He gave his head a little shake. "Maybe you'd better make sure I understand the question."

She tossed her thick, chestnut-colored hair, tipping her chin to gaze up at him, pressing closer still, and he braced himself to hold them both steady.

"The question, Caleb Terrell, is do you want to make love with me?"

Before he could form a conscious thought, his lips swooped down on hers, kissing her deeply, drinking in her sweet, fresh taste. He bracketed her face with his hands, backing her against the hallway wall, letting his fingertips explore the satin of her skin, the softness of her hair. He kissed her a second time, and a third and a fourth, desperately wishing the moment could last forever.

When he finally forced himself to stop, all but shaking with the effort, he breathed deeply and drew back a few inches, gazing into her eyes. With the pad of his thumb, he smoothed her flushed cheek, drinking in her extraordinary beauty. When he spoke, his voice had dropped to a husky whisper. "The answer, Mandy Jacobs, is yes."

She smiled. "I couldn't stop thinking about you." Her arms twined around his neck. He hugged her close, lifting her from the floor, kissing her deeply, crossing the short distance to his bedroom.

Moonlight filtered through the window, while a glow of light cascaded in from the hallway. Caleb set her gently on her feet. She was wearing a plain, hunter-green T-shirt and soft, faded jeans. She'd discarded her boots, and her sock feet made her seem shorter than normal.

He pulled up from the hem of her T-shirt, slowly peeling it away from her body, popping it over her head to reveal a lacy, mauve bra.

"I love your underwear," he breathed.

She smiled, and her eyes glowed moss-green in the soft light.

He flicked open the snap of her jeans. "I want to see more of it." He slipped his hand beneath her waistband, leaning in for a gentle kiss, stroking his thumbs along the smooth softness of her skin. Her abdomen was flat, waist indented, hips gently rounded.

One palm strayed to the mound of her breast, cupping it through her bra, feeling the distinctive pebble beneath the wispy fabric.

She gasped in response, thrusting forward, and he circled the sensitive spot with his fingertip.

He tasted her neck, kissed his way along her shoulder, sliding her bra strap out of the way.

Her palms pressed against his bare chest, smoothing their way down to his belly, as he used his free hand to push down her zipper.

"You're overdressed." He tugged down her jeans, slipping them off along with her socks, tossing them all to the floor. Then he stared at her for a long minute, unable to drag his gaze from her perfection.

"You're making me self-conscious," she complained.

He reached out, grazing his knuckles over her navel. "Do you have any idea how gorgeous you are?"

"I'm a sturdy, little workhorse."

He grinned. "Not hardly." He slipped his hand beneath the low waist of her panties. "You're a sexy, sculpted fantasy come to life."

She met his gaze, and he could see her skepticism.

"That's not a line, Mandy." He toyed with the other bra strap, pushing it off her shoulder, staring at the picture she made, not quite believing it could be real.

With anticipation killing him, he drew her back into his arms, kissing her hot mouth, probing with his tongue, bending her backward. He tugged off the towel, then moved his hands to her bottom, pressing her close, feeling the silk of her panties against his bare skin.

Her hands went to his hairline at the back of his neck, her fingers burrowing their way upward. She kissed him back, deeply and thoroughly, small purrs forming deep in her throat.

He flicked the clasp of her bra, discarding it with the rest of her clothes, covering her bare breast with his palm, groaning at the intense sensation of her spiked nipple and the softness that molded to his fingertip.

"Tell me you have condoms," she breathed.

"Oh, yeah." There was no way he was stopping this time.

Her small fingers stroked the length of his chest, over his belly, across his thighs, closer and closer, until he hissed in a breath. "You are definitely killing me now."

He hooked his thumb in her panties, stripping them down, getting them off at least one ankle before he reveled in her nakedness pressed against his. His mouth zeroed in on her breasts, feasting on one and then the other.

She whispered his name, her hands convulsing against his hair. He lifted her, pressed her back onto the bed and stretched out beside her. He kissed and caressed the length of her body. She dampened his neck, his shoulder, his chest, kissing her way down his abdomen, until he stopped her, pressing her onto her back, moving over her, letting his weight move between her spread legs.

He took a second with the condom.

Their gazes locked, hers a clouded jade, his barely able to focus.

He brushed his thumb across her lower lip, dipping it inside the hot cavern of her mouth. She suckled, swirling her tongue across the sensitive pad.

He kissed her hard, and she arched her back, twisting her hands into the quilt.

"I'm sure," she gasped, and he arched forward.

The second he was inside her, a roaring need took over his brain. Desire pulsed to every point of his body. His hands roamed her breasts, his lips moved from her mouth, to her shoulder, tasting everything in between.

She was all motion beneath him, her breaths coming in small gasps, her body arching to meet his rhythm, her arms rigid, head tipped back and her eyes closed shut.

He lost track of time, sensation after sensation building

within him. He held on as long as he could. But when she cried out his name, and her small body convulsed, he followed her over the edge, oblivion washing over him in waves.

The roaring in his ears slowly subsided. Though his muscles were spent, he braced his elbows, worried that his weight might crush her. But he didn't want to move, didn't want to withdraw, didn't want real life crowding in on paradise.

When worry for her comfort trumped his longing, he moved off. But he bent one knee, laying his leg across her thighs, and he wrapped his arms around her, pulling her into the cradle of his body, resting a palm across her warm, smooth belly to keep the connection intact. "You're amazing," he whispered huskily in her ear.

"You're not so bad yourself."

"Glad to hear it." He kissed her lobe, thinking he could happily start all over again.

They breathed in sync for a few minutes, and even as reality returned, a strange sense of calm stole over him.

It was odd. This was still his childhood bedroom, still the family ranch. Three oil paintings of quarter horses hung on his wall. The scents of the fields wafted in the window. And the sounds of the animals punctuated the night.

But for some reason it felt softer, the edges didn't seem so sharp.

"What?" she asked, twisting her head to look at him in the half light.

"I didn't say anything."

"You sighed like the world was coming to an end."

"It's not."

"Are you upset?"

"No."

She moved to a sitting position, her expression pensive. "Regrets?"

"No." He vigorously shook his head, pulling her back down, wrapping an arm tightly around her. "Absolutely none."

She seemed to relax, and her fingertips brushed across his

chest, while her warm breath puffed on his neck. He burrowed against her thick hair and inhaled the clean, citrus scent.

"It's funny," he ventured. For some reason, he wanted to put the feeling into words. Unusual for him, but he plunged on. "This is the closest I've ever come to being content in this room."

"That's good." She twisted her neck to look up at him. "Do you think maybe we banished some demons?"

"Maybe," he allowed.

"I feel very powerful," she joked.

"Then again—" he kept it light "—it could be that you are the most fun I've had in this house since my mom made chocolate mint fudge on our eighth birthday."

She grinned. Then she sobered and drew back, eyeing him quizzically. "Wait a minute. Did I beat the fudge, or was it the other way around?"

"Not a fair comparison. Apples to oranges."

She socked him in the shoulder. "Man, did you ever miss that opportunity."

"Ouch. Sorry."

"You better be. Chocolate mint fudge. Like it could hold a candle to me."

"It could when I was eight."

"You're not making this better, Caleb."

He chuckled low.

"You know," she began, coming up on her knees. "We may be on to something here."

He reached for her, not wanting this space between them. "Oh, I think we are. And I think we should do it again."

She batted at his hand. "I meant, changing your perception of the ranch. Not just your bedroom. And not just with sex. But the whole thing."

Something cold settled into Caleb's stomach. Was she really going to turn this into a sell-the-ranch, don't-sell-the-ranch thing?

"I know exactly how we could do it," she rattled on, voice decisive.

"Mandy, don't—"

"You need to talk to Reed, *really* talk to Reed."

"How the hell did Reed get into this conversation?" Annoyance put an edge to Caleb's voice.

She stopped. She blinked.

He tried but didn't quite keep the edge out of his tone. "Last time I checked, it was just you and me in this bed."

"But… He's your brother."

"That means something completely different to you than it does to me."

Caleb knew his anger stemmed from disappointment. But what had he expected? He and Mandy were still the same people. They still had divergent goals. Nothing had fundamentally changed because they'd sweated naked in each other's arms.

She shook her head in response to his statement, her rich hair flowing with the motion. "No, it doesn't. This land, your family, Reed. They're all part of your history and your heritage. You couldn't erase them by running away when you were seventeen, and you can't erase them by selling out now."

His annoyance was growing to full-out anger. "I did *not* run away."

"Semantics." She waved a dismissive hand. "Why did you smash the picture?"

Caleb set his jaw but didn't answer. He'd smashed the picture because he couldn't stand to see his father's smug face staring out at him one minute longer.

"Why did you smash the picture?" she repeated.

"Drop it, Mandy."

Her tone turned softer. "If you didn't care anymore, you wouldn't have smashed the picture." She gave a heartfelt sigh. "Staying away for ten years didn't fix it, did it?"

"This is none of your business," he told her firmly. It was temporary, a blip on his radar. A few days—a few weeks, max—and he'd be back to his regular life in Chicago. The ranch would cease to exist for him. And that's the way he wanted it.

"Do you think you've been repressing your true feelings?"

Suddenly, Caleb simply felt tired. He didn't want to fight with her. Mandy was the sole bright spot in all this madness.

He reached for her, urging her back down into his arms, genuinely trying to see things from her perspective.

"If it makes you happy," he told her. "Yes, I've been repressing my feelings. My childhood sucked. Reed made a stupid choice from which our relationship will probably never recover. And, I'm sorry to have to be so blunt. But there's nothing you can do to help. I know you disagree, but I'm making the right choice."

"It's—"

He pressed his index finger across her warm, swollen mouth. "For me, Mandy. It's the right choice for me."

Her green eyes turned soft and sympathetic.

He forced out a smile. "But you've made it better for right now." He couldn't resist, so he kissed her mouth one more time. "You've made things much better for right now."

Desire surging, he wrapped an arm around her waist and pulled her close. She was instantly kissing him back, her soft, sinuous body wrapping itself around him one more time.

He made love to her slowly, gently, savoring every second of the peace she offered.

Afterward, they lay still and silent for a long time.

It was Mandy who finally broke it.

"I need to go home," she whispered.

His eyes came open. "Why?" He didn't want her to leave. He didn't want her to move an inch, at least until morning.

But she twisted her neck to look at him. "It's coming up on eleven."

"You have a curfew?"

"Travis looked pretty suspicious when I left."

"So?"

Travis's interference was definitely not welcome in this. Whatever was between Caleb and Mandy was none of her brother's business.

"So, if I come home after midnight, he's going to put two and two together."

"And?"

"And, he'll be upset."

Caleb propped himself on one elbow. "Are you telling me this was a clandestine fling?" Even as he said the words, he asked himself to come up with an alternative. What were they going to do? Date until he left for Chicago? Own up to her brothers that they'd slept together?

"I think that's the best way to handle it, don't you?"

"You're an adult," he reasoned out loud. "Your private life is none of your brother's business."

Mandy laughed. "You going to tell him that?"

Caleb was willing, if that's what Mandy wanted him to do.

"I could tell him," she mused with a nod. "But then there'd be a fight."

"I'm not afraid of Travis." Caleb had no intention of lying about his relationship with Mandy.

"I meant with me, not you. And, with everything else going on, I really don't have the energy to fight Travis."

"I don't like this," said Caleb. He wanted her to stay right where she was. He wanted to hold her in his arms all night long, maybe even beyond that.

She cocked her head, defying his mood by giving him a saucy grin. "A few minutes ago, you seemed to like it just fine."

"I don't want to go sneaking around behind your family's back."

She patted his chest. "For now, let's just keep it quiet. Who knows what happens next between us. Maybe nothing."

Caleb was hoping for a lot more than nothing.

"If you go ahead with your plan to sell, you know you could be gone in a matter of days," she reasoned. There was no inflection to her tone, impossible to tell if she'd miss Caleb or not.

Then she gave a wry half smile. "You want to start world war three over something this insignificant?"

Insignificant?

"Because, believe me, Caleb, Travis is as overprotective as they come." She glanced at her watch. "I go home now, he can wonder, but he won't know. And if he doesn't know, he can't go off the deep end."

Caleb ran his fingers through her messy hair. "This is a stupid plan."

"But it's my plan." This time, there was a distinct edge to her voice. "Some decisions you get to make, Caleb. This one is mine."

He stared at the determination in her green eyes.

"Okay," he finally agreed. He'd keep the secret. Lady's choice. And he didn't kiss and tell.

The lights were on, and Travis was still up when Mandy came through the front door of the Jacobses' ranch house. He appeared in the kitchen doorway, a screwdriver in one hand, a rag in the other.

He stared at her for a long, silent minute as she tugged off her boots and tucked her loose hair behind her ears.

He took two steps forward. "Tell me you didn't."

"Didn't what?" She steeled herself for a moment then met his gaze full-on.

"Mandy." He smacked the screwdriver and rag on top of the dining-room table. "He'll break your heart."

"I have no idea what you're talking about." She had her suspicions, but she didn't know for sure, so it wasn't a lie.

"What do I always tell you?" He came forward at an angle, giving her the impression he was circling in.

"You're going to have to be a little more specific."

"We're not like you, Mandy. We're guys. We'll say anything, do anything—"

"Caleb's not like that."

Travis scoffed out a cold laugh. "What did he tell you?"

"He didn't tell me anything. And I don't know what you're talking about." She stomped to the sofa and flopped down, picking up this month's *Equestrian* magazine and opening it in front of her. "And I really don't want to have this conversation with you."

Travis moved to the armchair across from her. "He's from Chicago, Mandy. He's not staying."

"Don't you think I know that?" Mandy didn't expect Caleb to stay. Her wildest wish was that he'd hang around long enough to meet up with Reed. Beyond that, she had absolutely no illusions.

"The women he goes out with," Travis continued. "They know the score. They expect the lies. They know they're lies."

"Caleb has not lied to me."

"Then how'd he get you into bed."

Mandy determinedly flipped her way through the pages of the magazine. "None of this is any of your damn business."

"I love you, Mandy."

"Shut up."

"He doesn't."

She glanced over the top of the magazine. "What a ridiculous thing to say. Of course he doesn't love me. Why would he love me?"

"Then why won't you believe I have your best interest at heart?"

"I'm not a child, Travis. I like Caleb. Caleb likes me. Despite your cynicism, that's all there is to it. I'm not about to get hurt. And that's all you need to know."

"Then, why were you up there tonight?"

"He needs help," Mandy answered honestly.

"And you're going to be his Florence Nightingale?"

"He needs to see Reed. The two of them need to talk, really talk. You don't know what they went through as children." She breathed deeply, absolutely sincere in her argument.

Travis sat back, his posture relaxing. "I have a pretty good idea what they went through. I knew them both quite well."

Mandy dropped the magazine and sat forward. "Then help me find Reed. Caleb is determined to sell the ranch out from under him. He almost did it while we were in Lyndon. If I hadn't spoken up about the water rights, we might already have new neighbors. Reed needs the ranch, and Caleb needs Reed."

"You spoke up about the water rights review?"

"Yes."

"To Caleb's potential buyer?"

She paused. "It came up in conversation."

"And you think Caleb still likes you?" Reed asked on a note of astonishment.

"He understood."

"Mandy, the world isn't the happy fun place you seem to picture. People aren't sweet and kind and friendly, looking to do each other favors 24/7."

"Will you stop?"

"Reed and Caleb are grown men," Travis warned her darkly. "Neither of them is going to thank you for interfering."

Well, at least Danielle was on her side. She'd definitely thank Mandy for interfering.

"What if it was you?" Mandy asked. "What if you and Seth were estranged? Would you not want someone to facilitate your reunion? If you were about to lose the ranch, would you not want someone to help you out?"

Travis moved from the armchair and angled himself next to Mandy on the sofa. "Those two men have a very dark past. They're not going to recognize what you're doing as helpful. They're going to hate you for interfering."

"Reed would never hate me." And she had to believe Caleb wouldn't, either. Oh, she was under no illusion that he was falling for her in a romantic sense. But he had been a gentleman, more than a gentleman.

"Reed's been hurt pretty bad."

"Yes, he has," Mandy agreed. She paused, looking directly

at the brother she'd loved all her life. "And he's our friend. Do you really want me to turn my back on him?"

Travis mouthed a swearword, rocking back on the sofa. "You shouldn't be sleeping with Caleb, Mandy."

"I am not going to—"

"Stop talking right now," Travis barked. "Before you have to lie to me. If you fall for him, it's going to be a disaster." He paused, his mouth turning into a thin line. "Then again, if you're sleeping with him, it's already too late."

Mandy felt her throat close up with emotion. She couldn't think about her feelings for Caleb, not right now, not when so much was at stake. "I have to find Reed."

Travis hesitated, then he reached out and rubbed her shoulder. "Okay, little sister. Okay. I'll help you find Reed."

"You will?" she managed.

"I will."

"Good." She nodded, feeling stronger already. "Great. Danielle gave me a name—"

Travis recoiled. "Danielle?"

"Yes. She wants Reed to come back, so that Caleb will go back to Chicago. There's some Brazilian deal with a ticking clock." Mandy waved a dismissive hand. "Anyway. She put me in touch with a private investigator. And he's going to find Reed for us. All we have to do is keep Caleb from selling the ranch until then."

Eight

Caleb gazed up and down the wide hallway of the main Terrell barn, overwhelmed by the magnitude of the job in front of him. He'd had his secretary calling moving and storage companies this morning, but they all said they needed an estimate of the volume to be moved and stored. So Caleb had to figure out what to keep and store, and what to sell with the ranch.

He couldn't see the point of keeping the saddles and tack. Those things they'd sell as is. They'd also sell the horses and livestock. Same with the equipment and the vehicles. Whoever bought the ranch would likely have a use for much of the equipment, and Caleb was inclined to give them a good deal if it meant streamlining the sale.

The office—now, that was a different story. His boots thumped against the wooden floor as he crossed the aisle to stare in the open door of the office. It held two desks, five file cabinets and a credenza that stretched under the window. Some of the paperwork would stay, but a lot of it would be personal and business records that would have to be kept for the family. Well, for Reed. And that meant sorting through everything.

Caleb let his shoulders slump, turning his back on that particular job and making his way farther into the barn. About twenty horses were stabled inside. He made a mental note to make sure the hands were exercising each of them every day. He'd spoken briefly to their half dozen full-time hands, the cook and with the two men who were up from the Jacobses' place.

Everything was at least under temporary control.

A horse whinnied in one of the stalls, drawing Caleb's attention. He took a step closer, squinting into the dim stall.

"Neesha?" he asked, recognizing the Appaloosa mare. "Is that really you?"

She bobbed her head, seeming to answer his question.

A beauty, she was chestnut in the front, with just a hint of a white blaze. Her hindquarters were mottled white above a long, sleek tail.

She lifted her head over the stall, and he scratched her nose, rubbing her ears. She'd been a two-year-old when he left, one of the prettiest foals ever born on the ranch. He glanced into tack room, realizing her saddle and bridle would be easy to find using his father's ultra-organized system. He also realized he'd love to take her out for a ride.

Someone entered through the main door, heavy steps, long strides, booted feet, likely one of the hands.

"Caleb?" came Travis's flat voice.

Caleb's hands dropped to the top rail, fingers tensing around the rough board. He was under no illusion that Mandy could keep up a lie to her brother. So, if Travis had pressed her last night, he was likely here looking to take Caleb out behind the barn.

Caleb braced himself and turned.

Travis came to a halt, but when he spoke, there was no malice in his voice. "I guess it's been a while since you saw Neesha."

"It's been a while," Caleb agreed, watching Travis carefully. A sucker punch was no less than he deserved.

"You up to something?" asked Travis.

Caleb had no idea how to answer that question.

"Hear from any new buyers?" Travis tried again.

"Nothing so far." Caleb allowed himself to relax ever so slightly. Perhaps Mandy was more devious than he'd given her credit for.

"I'm trying to get an estimate for moving and storage." His gaze was drawn past the big double door, toward the ranch house. He couldn't begin to imagine how big a job it would be sorting through the possessions in the house. In addition to the rooms, there was the attic, the basement. He'd like to think he was emotionally ready to tackle it, but a thread of uncertainty had lodged itself in his brain.

Travis nodded. "A lot of years' worth of stuff in there."

"It's a bitch of a situation," said Caleb.

"That it is," Travis agreed. "We've got to ride the north meadow fence today. You up for it?"

"With you?"

"With me."

For a brief second, Caleb wondered if Travis was luring him away from the homestead in order to do him harm. But he quickly dismissed the suspicion. If Travis wanted to take his head off, he'd have tried by now. From everything Caleb knew and had learned, the man was tough as nails, but he wasn't devious.

"Sure," Caleb agreed. The house could wait. It wasn't as though it was going anywhere.

"I'll take Rambler," said Travis.

The two men tacked up the horses and exited into the cool morning sunshine. The meadow grass was lush green, yellow-and-purple wildflowers poking up between leaves and blades, insects buzzing from plant to plant, while several of the horses in the paddock whinnied their displeasure at being left behind.

They went north along the river trail, bringing back Caleb's memories of his childhood, and especially his teenage years. He, Reed and Travis had spent hours and hours on horseback out in the pastures and rangeland. They'd had a special clearing by the river, where they'd hung a rope swing. There, they'd swam in the frigid water, drank beer they'd bribed the hands to bootleg for them, bragged about making out with the girls at school and contemplated their futures. Funny, that none of them ever planned to leave the valley.

"I did a search on Active Equipment," Travis offered, bringing Rambler to walk alongside Neesha. "You've been busy."

"Had nothing better to do," Caleb responded levelly, though he was proud of his business achievements.

Travis chuckled. "I bet you fly around the world in that jet, going to parties with continental beauties, while your minions bring in the millions."

"That's pretty much all there is to it." Caleb pulled his hat down and bent his head as they passed beneath some low-hanging branches. He was surprise by how natural it felt to be in the saddle.

"Gotta get me a job like that."

Caleb turned to look at Travis. "Are you thinking of leaving Lyndon Valley?"

"Nah, not really. Though I wouldn't mind tagging along on one of your trips sometime, maybe Paris or Rome. I hear the women are gorgeous."

"Open invitation. Though, I have to warn you, it's mostly boardrooms and old men who like to pontificate about their social connections and their financial coups."

"You're bursting my bubble."

"Sorry."

They were silent while the horses made their way down a steep drop to a widening in the river. There, they waded hock-deep to pick up the trail at the other side, where they climbed to the flat.

"You remember the swing?" asked Travis.

"I remember," Caleb acknowledged. If they turned north and followed the opposite riverbank, instead of veering across the meadow, they'd be there in about ten minutes.

"You remember when Reed dislocated his shoulder?"

Caleb found himself smiling. It was the year they were fifteen. Reed's arm had snagged on the rope, yanking his shoulder out of his socket as he plummeted toward the deep spot in the river. He'd shrieked in pain as he splashed in, but he'd been able to swim one-armed through the frigid water back to shore.

Fresh off a first-aid course in high school, Caleb and Travis managed to pop the shoulder back into place.

"He never did tell my dad," Caleb put in.

Caleb had helped his brother out with his chores as best he could for the next few weeks, but Reed had pretty much gritted his teeth and gutted it out.

"I thought it was funny at the time," said Travis. "But five years ago, I dislocated my own shoulder. Codeine was my best friend for about three days. Your brother is one tough bugger."

Caleb knew Reed was tough. Reed had been taller and stronger than Caleb for most of their lives. He'd uncomplainingly taken on the hardest jobs. When Caleb had become exhausted and wanted to quit, risking their father's anger, Reed was the one who'd urged him on, one more hay bale, one more board, one more wheelbarrow load. He would not quit until he'd finished an entire job.

"And he never backed down from a fight," said Travis.

Caleb stilled. He let his mind explore some more of the past, remembering the day he'd walked away from the ranch. For the first time, it occurred to him that Reed probably saw leaving as backing down, and staying behind as a way of holding his ground against their father. He'd wanted Caleb to stay, begged him to stay, asked Caleb to stand toe to toe with him when it came to Wilton.

"And he hasn't changed," Travis continued. "It's a little harder to make him mad now, but once you do, stand back."

Caleb knew he'd made Reed angry. Back then he'd done it by walking away. Now he'd done it all over again by inheriting the ranch. It didn't matter that he was right. It didn't matter that Reed was misguided. The damage was done.

An image of his brother's mulish, teenage expression flashed into Caleb's brain. His throat suddenly felt raw. He knew a line had been drawn in the dust. He also knew he was never going to see his brother again.

He pressed his heels into the mare and leaned forward in the saddle, urging her from a walk to a trot to a gallop. He heard Travis's shout of surprise, and then Rambler's hooves pounded behind them.

The world flashed past, Neesha's long strides eating up the ground, her body strong beneath him, her lungs expanding, breaths blowing out. He settled into the rhythm, breathing deep, fighting to clear his mind of memories.

But the memories wouldn't stop. He saw Reed when they were seven, wrestling on their beds when they were supposed to be asleep, their father's shouts from the living room, the two of them diving under their covers, and lying stock-still while they waited to hear Wilton's footsteps on the stairs.

He saw them chasing down an injured calf when they were thirteen, waving their arms, yelling until they were hoarse, corralling it where they could look at the gash on its shoulder. Reed had held it still, while Caleb applied antibiotic ointment and crudely stitched the wound.

Unfortunately, their efforts had only served to make their father angry. He told them they'd wasted far too much time and effort on a single calf and made them work an extra two hours before allowing them to come in for a cold dinner.

But there were also good times, when Wilton had been out on the range, sometimes for days at a time. When their mother would relax and smile, and they'd play board games, watch silly sitcoms and eat hamburgers on the living-room sofa. Reed had been there for the good times and the bad. They'd struggled through homework together, commiserated with each other over unfair punishments, drank illicit beer, raced horses and teased each other mercilessly at every opportunity.

Travis shouted from behind him, and Caleb saw they were coming up on the fence-line. He pulled back on the reins, slowing the mare to a walk, forcing deep breaths into his tight lungs.

"You going for a record?" Travis laughed as he caught up. Both horses were breathing hard, sweat foaming out on their haunches.

"Haven't done that in years," Caleb managed without looking in Travis's direction.

"It's like riding a bike."

"Tell that to my ass." Caleb adjusted his position.

Travis laughed at him. "And we're going all the way around Miles Butte."

"That'll take all day." And half the night. "We'll be lucky to get home by midnight."

"You got something you have to do?" Travis watched Caleb a little too carefully, waiting for his answer.

Yes, Caleb had something he wanted to do. He wanted to see Mandy again.

But, apparently, Travis wasn't about to let that happen.

Mandy hadn't seen Caleb in two days. She'd read in one of Abigail's women's magazines that if a man wasn't into you, there was little you could do to attract him. But if a man *was* into you, he was like a heat-seeking missile, and nothing would slow him down.

Caleb definitely wasn't a heat-seeking missile. And it had occurred to her more than once over the past two days that he might have got what he wanted from her and now moved on. Maybe Travis was right, and that was the way they did it in Chicago.

Even this morning, they were taking two vehicles from the ranch to Lyndon for the first water rights review meeting. Seth, Abby and Mandy ended up in the SUV, while Travis and Caleb drove the pickup truck. It wasn't clear who had orchestrated the seating arrangements, but surely any self-respecting heat-seeking missile could have managed to get into a vehicle with her.

Mandy tried not to focus on Caleb as they turned off the highway onto Bainbridge. There was plenty to be optimistic about between her father's continuing progress at the rehab clinic in Denver and Seth getting more and more excited about the upcoming campaign. He and Abigail had been discussing and debating political issues all the way from the ranch to Lyndon. And, with Seth and their father pretty much out of the picture, Travis seemed to be relishing his new role as de facto ranch manager.

Not that Mandy was jealous.

Though, now that she thought about it, everyone in her family seemed to be moving into some kind of new phase in their lives. Except for her. Other than supporting Travis at home, finding Reed and getting the Terrell family back on track, what was next for her?

"Mandy?" Abby interrupted her thoughts from the front passenger seat.

"Hmm?"

"Can you check my briefcase back there? I want to make sure I brought all five copies of the information package."

Mandy reached for the briefcase where it was sitting on the SUV floor, pulling it by the handle to lay it flat on the seat beside her. She snapped the clasps and pulled it open.

"The green books?" she asked, thumbing her way through the rather professional-looking coil-bound, plastic-covered volumes."

"Those are the ones."

Mandy counted through the stack to five. "They're all here."

"Thanks," Abby sang. Then she turned her attention to Seth. "I've got us all at the Sunburst. You're sharing with Travis, and I'm with Mandy. I put Caleb on his own. I figured, you know, the big, bad, Chicago executive might not be used to sharing a bathroom."

Seth laughed, but Mandy couldn't help remembering that

Caleb had shared a bathroom with her at the Rose Inn. He'd seemed perfectly fine with that. Then again, they'd been trapped in a storm. It could be considered an emergency situation. But he'd worked like a dog for the next three days. And he hadn't complained in the slightest about the accommodation, the food or the hard work. He didn't strike her as somebody who required creature comforts.

She opened her mouth to defend him, but then changed her mind. She really shouldn't be thinking so much about Caleb. She should be thinking about Reed, and how to find him, and how soon she could reasonably touch base with Enrico Rossi and check the status of his investigation. Or maybe she could call Danielle directly. Perhaps she'd heard something from Enrico.

Seth pulled into the parking lot at the side of the Sunburst Hotel. Travis's pickup truck was already parked, and he and Caleb were getting out. Mandy watched Caleb's rolling, economical movements as he pulled a small duffel bag from the box of the pickup truck. His gaze zeroed in on the SUV, finding hers as he strode across the parking lot toward them.

She quickly looked away and concentrated on climbing out the back door. He swung open the back hatch and began loading his arms with their luggage. Travis followed suit. Seth grabbed the last bag, and beeped the SUV lock button. Mandy was left with nothing but her shoulder bag to carry into the lobby.

Caleb fell into step beside her.

"How're you doing?" he rumbled.

"Just fine," she told him primly, concentrating her focus on the short set of concrete steps that led into the glass entrance.

A set of double glass doors slid silently open in front of them, welcoming them into the gleaming high-ceilinged, marble-floored, floral-decorated lobby. Pillars formed a big circle around a patterned tile floor, while the service desks formed an outer ring in front of the walls.

"I've got a copy of the confirmation," Abby announced, slipping a sheaf of papers from a side pocket in her bag.

"Let me get the check-in." Seth strode up to a uniformed woman at the registration desk.

Caleb lengthened his strides after Seth, leaving Mandy behind. He caught up and put his credit card on the counter. Seth immediately shoved the card back toward Caleb. The two men had a brief debate, and it looked like Seth was the one to back off.

Mandy positioned herself beside a pillar, out of the route of direct walking traffic, next to Abigail and the luggage.

A few minutes later, Caleb returned to them.

"Ladies." He nodded. "I assume these are your bags?" He scooped up their suitcases.

"Those are ours," Abigail confirmed.

"Then, right this way. You're on the tenth floor. As am I, and Caleb and Seth are on seven."

"One second," said Abigail, finding a glass-topped table to set down her briefcase.

She opened it, pulled out two of the green packages and took a few steps across the lobby to hand them to Travis. "Lunch is at the Red Lion next door. The meeting starts at one o'clock. We have dinner reservations at the Riverfront Grill. And then I thought we'd go to the Weasel." She did a little shimmy as she mentioned the name of the most popular dancing bar in Lyndon. "It's Friday night, so they'll have a band."

Travis took the books from her hands, giving her a mock salute. "Works for me. See you guys in a few."

Caleb headed for the elevator, and Mandy fell into step behind him.

On the tenth floor, they exited, finding their room five doors down. Abby inserted the key card, holding the door open for Caleb with the bags. Mandy brought up the rear.

"This looks nice," Caleb noted politely, setting the bags on the padded benches at the foot of each of the queen-size beds. The room had a small sitting area near a bay window with a view of the town. The two beds looked thick and comfortable, and the bathroom appeared clean, modern and spacious.

"I'll see you both at lunch," he finished, heading for the door.

He opened it, got halfway out and then stopped, turning back. "Mandy? You have a minute? I've got something I want to ask you about, but it's buried in the bottom of my bag." He gestured into the hallway. "You mind?"

Surprised and confused, and worried it might have something to do with the sale of the ranch, Mandy nodded. "Uh, sure. No problem." She moved after him, telling herself it couldn't be a sale. Not this fast. Not without any warning.

"Great." He flashed a smile at Abigail. "Thanks."

Outside in the hallway, they moved three doors farther down. Caleb inserted his own key card, opening the door to a larger room with a king-size bed and a massive lounge area beside a pretty bay window.

They entered the room. He dropped his bag on the floor. The spring-loaded door swung shut and, before she knew what was happening, Mandy was up against the back of the closed door. Caleb's hands had her pinned by her wrists, and he was kissing her hard and deep.

She was too stunned to move. "What the—"

"I've been going crazy," he groaned between avid kisses. "You're making me crazy. I thought we'd never get here. I thought we'd never get checked in. I thought we'd never get a second alone."

Mandy recovered her wits enough to kiss him back. So, not the sale of the ranch. And okay, this was definitely a heat-seeking missile.

She relaxed into the passion of his kisses.

His lips moved to her neck, pulling aside her shirt. A rush of desire tightened her stomach, tingling her skin. Her eyes fluttered closed and her head tipped back, coming to rest against the hard plane of the door as her toes curled inside her boots.

"I don't understand," she managed to mutter, clinging to

his arms to balance herself. "You've ignored me for two days. I didn't hear a word."

"That was Travis. He used every trick in the book to keep me away from you." Caleb pulled back. "What did you tell him, by the way?"

"I didn't... Well, I mean, I didn't *tell* him. But he knows."

"Yeah, he knows," Caleb agreed. "But can we talk about your brother later? I figured we've got about three minutes before they come looking for us."

She blinked at him in astonishment. "You don't mean?"

"Oh, man. I *wish*. But, no. I was only planning to kiss you some more."

The regional water rights review meeting was shorter than Mandy had anticipated. The state representative introduced the process and told participants how they could provide written comments in advance of the next meeting. Having five people attend from the Jacobs and Terrell families, along with dozens of other ranchers from the Lyndon Valley area served its purpose in showing the organizers the level of interest from the valley and from the ranching community.

There were also a number of people representing nonranching interests. That had been one of Seth and Abigail's concerns, that ranchers might be pushed out as the area tried to attract newer industries.

Caleb asked questions, and Mandy was impressed with both his understanding of the process and his ability to zero in on the significant details. If she found Reed, and if he returned to the ranch, she hoped Caleb would stay involved until the end of the review. Even if he had to do it from Chicago.

As the meeting broke up, and the group made their way toward the doors of the town hall, Abigail linked an arm with Mandy. "Did you bring along a dress for tonight?"

"A what?"

"A dress. You know, that thing that replaces pants on formal occasions."

Mandy gave her sister a look of incredulity. "No, I didn't bring a dress." Why on earth would she bring a dress? This was a community meeting. In Lyndon.

"Well, we've got a couple of hours before dinner. Let's go to the mall and be girls for a while."

Mandy glanced over her shoulder at Caleb. She'd been hoping to steal a few more minutes alone with him before they all convened for dinner. "I'm not sure—"

"Come on. It'll be fun." Abigail raised her voice. "Wouldn't you guys like to escort two gorgeous women out on the town tonight?"

Travis stepped up. "Why? You know some?"

She elbowed him. "Mandy and I are going for a makeover."

"Great idea," said Travis, voice hearty. "You two ladies take your time. Have fun."

Mandy shot Caleb a helpless look.

He came back with a shrug that clearly stated "see what I mean?"

"Fine," Mandy capitulated, mustering up some enthusiasm, even as she wondered whether Travis had co-opted her sister to the cause of keeping her and Caleb apart.

"I haven't been in Blooms for ages," said Abigail, towing Mandy toward the SUV. She called back over her shoulder. "You guys okay to walk back to the hotel?"

Seth waved them off. "We'll see you at the restaurant."

Abigail hit the unlock button for the vehicle, and its lights flashed twice. "They can go find a cigar bar or something."

"Did Travis put you up to this?" Mandy asked across the roof of the vehicle.

Abigail gave her a blank look. "What do you mean? Why would Travis care what we do?"

Mandy peered closely at her sister. Abigail wasn't the greatest liar in the world. And she always had been much more interested in hair, makeup and fashion than Mandy. Maybe this was some kind of a bizarre coincidence.

"So, you just want to go shopping?"

"No," said Abigail. "I want to go shopping, hit the hair salon and get our makeup and nails done. I'd also suggest a facial, but I don't think we have that kind of time."

"Fine." Mandy threw up her hands in defeat. "Let's go be girls."

Abigail grinned and hopped into the driver's seat.

They drove the five miles to Springroad Mall, parked next to the main entrance, stopped to make sure the salon could fit them in later in the afternoon, then made their way through the main atrium to Blooms, the town's biggest high-end ladies' wear store. It occurred to Mandy that the last thing she'd purchased here was a prom dress.

"Something with a kick," said Abby, leading the way past office wear and lingerie. "I want a little lift in my skirt when I'm dancing."

"What happened to you in Denver?" Mandy couldn't help asking.

"I realized life was short," Abigail responded without hesitation. "I should be out there having fun and meeting people. So should you." She stopped in front of a rack of dresses.

"I'm really interested in the campaign," Abigail continued. "But I'll admit, at first, I wasn't crazy about the idea of spending so much time in Lyndon and Denver. But now I'm really looking forward to it. I'm going to stretch my wings."

Suddenly, Mandy become worried. "You're not planning to leave the ranch, are you?" They'd already lost one sister to the bright lights of a big city.

"Of course not. Not permanently, anyway. But I do want to test other waters. And this seems like a good time to do it." She held up an emerald-green dress. "What do you think? Does the color go with my hair?"

Abigail's hair was shoulder length and auburn. Colors could be challenging for her, but the green was perfect.

"Absolutely," Mandy replied.

A salesclerk arrived, offering to start a dressing room for

each of them. She took Abigail's choice of the green dress, and they moved on to the next rack.

Abigail quickly selected another. "You should go for red," she exclaimed, holding up a short, V-necked, cinnamon-red dress. It had black accents and a multilayered skirt that would swirl when she danced.

"Oh, sure," Mandy drawled sarcastically. "That looks just like me."

"That's the point. 'You' are blue jeans and torn T-shirts. We need to find something that is completely not you."

"My T-shirts aren't torn," Mandy protested. Okay, maybe one or two of them were, but she wore those only when she was mucking out stalls or painting a fence.

Abigail waved the dress at the salesclerk, who promptly took it from her arms and whisked it off to the dressing room.

Abigail's next choice was basic black. She considered one with a sequined bodice, but discarded it. Mandy had to agree. They were going to the Weasel. It was a perfectly respectable cowboy bar, but it wasn't a nightclub.

They ended up with four dresses each. Mandy considered they were all too formal, but her sister seemed to be having such a good time, she didn't want to be the wet blanket.

In her dressing room, she put off the red dress to the very last. She tried a strapless, straight-skirted design in royal blue, but they all agreed the neckline didn't work. Then a basic black cocktail dress, which was too close to one of the few she already owned. Then she tried a patterned, empire-waist, knee-length concoction, with cap sleeves and a hemline ruffle. It made her look about twelve. Abigail actually laughed when she walked out to model it.

Abigail had already decided to go with the green, so she was waiting in her regular clothes when Mandy exited the dressing room in the red dress.

Her grin was a mile wide. "It's stunning," she pronounced.

The salesclerk nodded her agreement. "I wish I had legs

like that," she commented, looking Mandy up and down. "It fits you perfectly."

Mandy glanced to her legs. She didn't see anything particularly interesting about them. They held her up, helped her balance on a horse and could walk or jog for miles when necessary. That's all that counted.

"You probably want to shave them before we go out."

"Thanks tons, sis."

"But I've never seen you look so beautiful," Abigail declared. "You absolutely *have* to get it."

"I don't know when I'll ever wear it again," Mandy glanced at the price tag. It was about three times as much as she'd ever spent on a dress before.

"Well, you'll wear it tonight," said Abigail.

"And after that?"

"After that, who knows. You're about to become the sister of the Mayor of Lyndon."

The salesclerk gave Abigail a curious look.

"Our brother Seth Jacobs is running for mayor this fall," Abigail put in smoothly. "Make sure you vote."

"There'll be the swearing-in dance," the clerk offered to Mandy. "And that's always formal."

"We're only going to the Weasel tonight," Mandy noted, considering different angles in the mirror.

Okay, so the dress did look pretty darn good. It accentuated her waist. It would twirl enticingly while she danced. And it showed just enough cleavage to be exotic without being tacky. She wouldn't mind Caleb seeing her in this.

Behind her, in the mirror, the salesclerk waved a dismissive hand. "You can wear anything to the Weasel. Lots of the younger girls dress up to go there, especially on a Friday night."

"There you go," said Abigail. She glanced at her watch.

"You'd better made a decision quick because we have to get to the Cut and Curl."

Mandy drew a breath. Okay. The red dress it was. Her lips curled into an involuntary smile. "You talked me into it."

Nine

If Mandy was trying to drive Caleb stark raving mad, she was certainly going about it the right way. Her hair was up. Her heels were high. And the professionally applied makeup had turned her face from beautiful to stunning.

Her sassy red dress was enough to give a man a coronary.

When they walked into the Weasel, he hadn't even bothered asking her to dance, simply swirled her out onto the crowded dance floor and wrapped her tightly in his arms, before anybody else could get their hands on her. Since then, he'd been shooting warning glares at any guy who dared look twice.

Abigail was also quick to attract her share of partners. Caleb and Seth parked it at the bar, ordering up a round of beers.

Once he recovered the power of speech, Caleb put his lips close to Mandy's ear, keeping the volume of his voice just above the music of the country band. "You look gorgeous."

"You like?" she asked.

"I love."

She grinned at him, showing straight, white teeth, while her eyes flashed emerald. "Abby made me buy it."

"Abigail's my new favorite person."

"She'll be thrilled to hear it."

He spun Mandy around, then smoothly pulled her back against his body. "You should do this more often."

"Dance with you?"

"Well, yeah. That, too. But I meant dress up."

She arched a brow. "Something wrong with my blue jeans?"

"Don't be so sensitive. I prefer silk to denim on my dates. Deal with it."

"Well, I prefer blue jeans to suit jackets."

Caleb frowned at her. Then he made a show of glancing around the crowd. "Any casually dressed guy in particular catch your eye? I could dance you over and let him cut in."

"Sure," she teased right back. "What about the guy in the yellow hat?"

Caleb shook his head. "Looks a little too old for the likes of you."

"The one with the red boots?"

"Too short."

"Well…" She continued to scan the room before returning her attention to him. "Okay, what about you?"

"I'm wearing a suit. And I'm already dancing with you."

"A girl, Caleb. Pick out a girl. Who looks good to you?"

He kept his eyes fixed firmly on her. "I'm dancing with her."

"That's a cop-out."

"It's the truth. If there are any other girls in this room, I didn't notice."

"Smooth talker," she told him, but their gazes locked and held.

"What are you doing later?" he rumbled.

"I'm rooming with my sister."

"This is ridiculous," he griped, frustrated by the barriers that kept flying up in their way. "I feel like we're in high school."

"You think if it wasn't for Abigail, I'd be jumping into bed with you?"

Her question surprised and embarrassed him. Was he being presumptuous? Had he been that far wrong in reading her signals? Had he imagined her response to his lovemaking?

Sure, they'd argued afterward, but then they'd made love again. And she'd been all he could think of ever since, despite the fact Travis had kept him away from the ranch and out of cell range for two long days.

Did Mandy feel differently?

"I'm sorry," he began, feeling like a heel. "I didn't mean—"

"That's the problem, Caleb." Her look was frank. "I don't know what you mean. I just spent two days wondering what you mean."

"What I mean is that I like you, Mandy," he answered her as honestly as he could. "I like you a lot. I think you're beautiful and exciting and real. And I can't seem to get enough of you. I want to spend every minute in your company." His voice rose in frustration. "And I want to ditch all of your siblings so they'll stop getting in my way."

She broke into a smile. "That was a good answer."

"Thank you," he grumbled.

"But it's okay if you just think I'm sexy."

"I think you're that, too."

Her expression sobered. "When I didn't hear from you, I thought maybe once was enough."

"Twice," he corrected.

"Twice is enough?"

"No! I meant we did it twice already." He gathered her closer, adding some intimacy to the conversation by putting his mouth closer to her ear. "Twice is definitely not enough."

"You want to pick a number?" There was a thread of laughter in her tone. "That'll keep me from guessing where this is going and when it's going to end."

"Fifty," he told her.

"Ambitious."

"Always."

The band ended the song with a pounding drum solo, and the lead singer announced they were taking a break.

Abigail appeared next to them, commandeering Mandy for the ladies' room, and Caleb wound his way toward the bar.

He ordered a beer.

Travis stepped up. "Make it two."

"Find someone to dance with?" asked Caleb.

"Not a problem. I went to high school with half the people here."

"I recognize a few faces." Caleb glanced around the room, seeing at least a dozen people he'd known as a teenager.

The bartender set two bottles of beer on the bar, and Caleb handed him a twenty. He and Travis turned to face the crowd, Caleb scanning for Mandy.

"I see the way you're looking at my sister." Travis took a long swig of his beer.

Again? Caleb *really* didn't want to have this conversation. "Every man in the room is looking at your sister."

"Every man in the room isn't dancing with her."

"Only because I won't let them."

Travis opened his mouth to respond.

But Caleb interrupted him, squaring his shoulders as he angled to face Travis. He was getting this over with here and now. "You've got to back off, man. She's a grown woman."

The piped in music throbbed through the speakers, and a few dancers took the floor again.

"You don't have a sister."

Caleb crossed his arms over his chest. "I don't. But that doesn't change anything."

"It would change your attitude."

"Let's assume my attitude is not going to change in the next five minutes."

Travis took another pull on his bottled beer. "Yeah, I know."

"She's a smart woman, Travis. She's realistic and self-confident, and I'm not pressuring her to do anything."

"I'm backing off," said Travis.

The statement surprised Caleb, leaving him at a loss for words. Thanking Travis didn't seem remotely appropriate. So, he took a drink instead.

Seth appeared from the crowd. "What's going on?"

Caleb shot Travis a sidelong glance, wondering what he was going to say to his brother.

"Not much," Travis responded with a shrug.

Seth signaled for a beer and parked himself next to Caleb, facing the room along with them. "I think we're going to have to keep an eye on our sisters tonight."

Travis coughed out a laugh. "You think?"

"I never think of them as particularly beautiful," Seth continued. "But they clean up pretty good."

It was Caleb's turn to laugh. "Your sisters are drop-dead gorgeous, Seth."

"I know," said Seth in some amazement. He scooped a handful of peanuts from the bowl on the bar. "I'm picturing them on the campaign trail."

"What trail?" Travis challenged. "You're running for mayor, not governor."

"There'll still be photo ops. What do you think? One on each arm?"

"You'll look like Hugh Hefner."

"Hmm," Seth mused. "Guess I'd better rethink that."

At the far side of the room, Mandy reappeared with Abigail.

Men immediately took notice, sending interested gazes and shifting themselves in the women's direction, some of them obviously setting up to make a move. Caleb abandoned his beer and pushed away from the bar, setting a direct course for Mandy. Seth and Travis could look out for Abigail. But Caleb wasn't letting Mandy out of his sight.

Back in the hotel room, Mandy stripped off her high shoes. Abigail followed suit, stretching her bare feet out on an ottoman in their compact sitting area.

"My feet are definitely not in shape for strappy sandals," Abigail complained.

"I hear you." Mandy flopped down on the opposite arm-chair, stretching out her own sore feet, sharing the ottoman. She liked to think she was pretty tough, but she'd definitely been defeated by a dance floor. By midnight, even a few more minutes in Caleb's arms hadn't been enough of an incentive to add an extra blister.

"Felt a little like Cinderella, though, didn't it?" asked Abigail.

"Tomorrow, we go back to cleaning the fireplace."

"Well, horse stalls," said Abigail. "At least, that's your fate. I've been getting away with a lot of office work lately."

"I hate the office work."

"Lucky for me."

Mandy plucked at the silky layers of her dress. "Do you think the campaign is going to keep you in Lyndon a lot?"

Abigail shrugged. "More than usual, for sure. Why?"

"It's been awfully quiet at home."

Abigail grinned at her. "You missed me?"

"I did," Mandy admitted. "With Mom and Dad staying at the rehab center, and you and Seth in Denver and Lyndon, and Travis always out on the range, it'll just be me at lunch and probably just me at dinner."

"I think Travis likes his new role," said Abby. "With no Dad and no Seth, he's going to have a lot more responsibility."

Mandy had to agree. Travis seemed very happy. Once again, she got the feeling she was the only one left behind.

"Are you suffering from empty-nest syndrome?" Abigail asked, compassion in her dark, hazel eyes.

"Maybe I am," Mandy realized. "Weird. I never thought about how much my life depended on the rest of the family being there. It's like nobody needs me anymore."

"The ranch can't run without you and Travis."

"Without Travis, maybe. But you're the one who does the paperwork. The foreman knows what to do day to day. The hands know what to do. I'm… Okay, this is depressing. I think the Terrells need me more than my own family."

Abigail's eyes narrowed. "The Terrells?"

"Getting Reed back." Mandy was surprised Abigail didn't immediately understand. "Caleb's off on this crazy 'sell the ranch' tangent, and Reed's lying low. And somebody has to knock some sense into the both of them."

Abby moved her feet to the floor and sat forward in her chair. "They're grown men, Mandy."

"That doesn't mean they have a brain between them."

"That doesn't make it your responsibility."

Mandy shook her head. Her sister wasn't getting this. How had nobody else noticed? "The universe is out of balance, Abby. It has been for ten years. I love Reed."

"We all love Reed."

"There you go. I can't abandon him at a time like this, can I? He's my third brother."

Abby's face winkled in consternation. "Do you think there's any chance." She paused, watching Mandy carefully. "Any chance at all that—I mean, right now—you're somehow substituting Reed for your own family."

"I'm not—"

Abigail held up a hand. "Hear me out. We're all busy. And you're feeling adrift. And along comes this very juicy family problem that you think you might be able to solve."

"A *juicy problem?* You think I'm getting some kind of emotional satisfaction out of Caleb Terrell threatening to sell his family's ranch?"

"I think you're like a moth to a flame. Someone's hurt? There's Mandy. Someone's upset? There's Mandy. Two people in a dispute? There's Mandy."

"You say that like it's a bad thing."

"It's not a bad thing. It's a great thing. And it's an important role, *in your own family.* But when you start franchising out, it's a problem."

"This is Reed Terrell, not some stranger I picked up on the street."

Abigail chuckled at that. "All I'm saying is don't get too invested in Reed and Caleb Terrell. This may not be a problem you can solve."

Mandy's hand clamped down on the padded arms of the chair. In her mind, failure was not an option. "I have to solve it."

"And, if you can't?"

Mandy wasn't going to think about that right now. Reed gone from the Valley forever? Someone other than the Terrells living down the road? And Caleb gone, with no reason to ever return.

She hated to admit it, even to herself, but she'd started hoping he'd reconnect with Lyndon Valley, maybe come back once in a while. He did have his own jet. And then, they could...could...

Okay. Shelving that thought for now.

Abigail was watching her expectantly. "And if you can't?" she repeated.

"If I can't get them to reconcile," Mandy responded breezily. "Then, that's that. Reed will move and life will go on."

There was a long pause. "Why don't I believe you?"

"Because you're naturally suspicious. You have that in common with Travis."

"Ha. I'm naturally fun and exciting." Abigail was obviously willing to let the argument go. "Did you see all the guys who asked me to dance down there?"

Mandy smiled at her sister's exuberance, forcing herself to relax again. "Green is definitely your color."

"I'm wearing it more often. Five of them asked for my number."

"Did you give it out?"

"Nah. I'm not particularly interested in cowboys. What about you?"

"Nobody asked for my number."

Abigail's dark eyes glowed with interest. "I think Caleb's already got your number."

Mandy felt her cheeks heat.

Abigail sat up straight, staring intently. "So, I'm not crazy. You are into him."

"He's a good guy," Mandy offered carefully.

"You just told me that he's trying to sell the ranch, and you're trying to stop him. That doesn't sound like a good guy."

Mandy's cheeks grew hotter still. "Okay," she allowed. "Aside from that particular character flaw, he's a good guy."

Caleb was misguided, that was all. She was confident he'd eventually see the light. Assuming she could keep him from selling the ranch between now and then.

"He's definitely hunky," said Abigail.

Mandy nodded. There was no point in pretending she was blind. "Sexy as they come."

"So?" Abigail waggled her brows. "Did he kiss you?"

Mandy hesitated, wondering how much, if anything, she dared share with her sister.

"He *did,*" Abigail cried in triumph. "When? Where? I want the details."

A few beats went by in silence.

"Are you *sure* you want the details?" Mandy asked, a warning tone in her voice.

"Yeah."

Mandy screwed up her courage. "Everywhere."

Abigail blinked in confusion. "What do you mean?"

"I mean, he kissed me *everywhere.*"

Abigail's eyes went round. "We're not talking geography, are we?"

Mandy shook her head, a secretive grin growing on her face.

"When?"

"Two days ago."

"At the ranch?"

"His ranch."

"You didn't?"

"We did."

Abby plunked back in her chair, her expression a study in shock.

"Then I didn't hear from him afterward." Mandy found the words rushing out of her. "And I thought, okay, that's it, he's from the big city, and it was a one-night stand, and I can handle it. But then we got here—"

"And he made that stupid excuse to take you down to his room."

"Yes."

"And?"

"And it was like no time had gone by. He grabbed me, kissed me, talked about going crazy for not seeing me." For Mandy, it had been both gratifying and confusing. Her emotions had done a complete one-eighty in the space of about ten seconds.

"So, why didn't he call you?"

"Out on the range. Out of cell service. Apparently Travis was keeping him busy, and he didn't have a chance to see me. He said he tried."

"And while you were dancing tonight?" asked Abigail. "Did he proposition you again?"

Mandy nodded. That appeared to be the thing about a heat-seeking missile. They didn't leave you guessing.

Abigail's brows went up. "And you're sitting here with me, because…?"

The answer to that was pretty obvious. "Because two of my brothers and my sister are in the same hotel, and I don't want to upset anyone."

"You think *I'll* be upset because you spend the night with Caleb?"

"I think you'll be… I don't know." Mandy tried to put it into words. "Disappointed?"

"You're twenty-three years old. Besides, you already did it once. You think my delicate sensibilities can't stand being five rooms away while you have a sex life?"

"And there's Travis."

"What's Travis got to do with this?"

"He warned Caleb to keep his hands off me."

Abigail sputtered out a laugh. "Grow up, Travis. It's none of his damn business."

"I know that. And you know that. And believe me, that's Caleb's opinion. But I don't want to upset Travis."

Abigail sat forward again. "Mandy, honey, this family's emotional health is not your responsibility. I'm not suggesting you sleep with Caleb or you don't sleep with Caleb. What I am suggesting, is that you make up your own mind. You're allowed to do that."

It wasn't as simple as Abigail made it out to be. In families, people had a responsibility to the group, they couldn't just selfishly think of themselves alone.

"You think that when I date a guy, I'm worrying about your opinion?" Abigail asked.

"Well, I'd never—"

"I don't. And neither does Travis when he's dating a woman. And you shouldn't, either. Now." Abigail brought her palms firmly down on her lap. "If the rest of us weren't here, what would *you* do?"

Mandy pondered her sister's question. If she had it to decide all on her own, remembering their lovemaking from last time, thinking about his words and her feelings on the dance floor, taking into account that Caleb was here only temporarily?

Mandy bit down on her lower lip.

Abigail waited.

"I'd already be down the hall in his room," she admitted. "I'd be with Caleb."

Abigail's grin was a mile wide.

Three minutes later, standing barefoot outside Caleb's hotelroom door, Mandy was forced to tamp down a swell of butterflies battering her stomach. She was pretty sure he'd be glad to see her, but there was no way to be positive. Other than to knock on his door.

Right.

She brushed her palms against the skirt of her red dress, took a deep breath, glanced both ways down the corridor and knocked.

After only a few seconds, Caleb opened the door. His expression registering surprise, but the surprise was followed quickly by a broad smile that lit the depths of his blue eyes.

He reached for her hand, tugging her quickly inside the room.

"Hey, Mandy," he whispered gruffly.

As the door swung shut behind her, his lips came down on hers in a long, tender kiss.

He pulled back, grin still firmly in place as he smoothed back her hair. "You're here."

She couldn't hold back her answering smile. "I am."

"Can you stay?"

She nodded, and he drew her into a warm, enveloping hug, wrapping his body possessively around her.

For some reason, she suddenly felt trapped. "Uh, Caleb?"

"Hmm?" he asked between kisses.

"I know you probably want to jump straight into bed."

He immediately pulled back again, his hands gently, loosely cupping her bare shoulders. "Hey, no."

There was genuine regret in his eyes. "I'm sorry about what I said earlier. That was presumptuous and disrespectful. You being here, in my room, doesn't mean anything you don't want it to mean." His words sped up. "Seriously, Mandy. No pressure."

Her heart squeezed with tenderness. "I'm not saying we shouldn't go to bed at all. I just thought, maybe first—"

"You want a glass of wine?" He took her hand and led her to the big sitting area at the far end of the huge, rectangular room. A big, bay window overlooked the river and the moon hung high above the mountains. It was a clear night, with layers of stars twinkling deep into space.

"Wine sounds good." She perched on one end of the couch.

"We can talk," he said as he moved to the wet bar, stopping to turn on some soft music, before returning with two glasses of red wine. "Merlot okay? I can order something else if you'd like."

She accepted the glass. "This'll be fine."

He sat down at the opposite end of the couch, leaving a wide space between them.

She leaned back, and their gazes locked for a long, breath-robbing minute. The air seemed to sizzle, and her skin broke out in goose bumps while her heart sped up, throbbing deep in her chest.

"Tell me about Chicago," she managed, hoping to keep from throwing herself at him for at least five minutes.

"What do you want to know?"

"Where do you live?" She took a sip of the robust, deep-flavored wine. It danced on her tongue, then warmed her extremities as she swallowed. Or maybe it was Caleb's presence that warmed her extremities. It was impossible to tell for sure.

"I have an apartment. It's downtown. On top of a thirty-five-story building."

"So, it's a penthouse?" That shouldn't have surprised her. But she found it was hard for her to get used to Caleb's level of wealth. Though the fact that he owned a jet plane should have made it clear.

"I guess you could call it that," he answered easily. "I bought it because it's close to our head office. The plants are all in in-dustrial parks in the outskirts of the city, but it makes sense to have the head office downtown."

"You don't have to apologize to me for having a downtown office."

He chuckled. "When I'm talking to you, it feels a little ex-travagant. Truth is, most of our international clients stay down-town, so it's for convenience as much as anything else. I'm not trying to impress anyone."

"I wouldn't think you'd have to try." She imagined people

would be impressed without Caleb having to lift a finger in that direction.

He gave a mock salute with his wine glass. "Was that sarcasm?"

"Truthfully, it wasn't. Though I am struggling to picture you with a list of international clients."

"That's why I'm forced to wear a suit. It helps them take me more seriously."

She smiled at his joke and drank some more wine, feeling much more relaxed than when she first walked in.

"We've had inroads into Canada and Mexico for quite some time," Caleb elaborated. "Our first expansion of a plant outside of the Chicago area was Seattle. With the port there, we had access to the Pacific Rim. It turned out to be a really good move. So, now, we have buyers from Japan, Korea, Hong Kong, as far away as Australia. That's when we bought the jet. We started doing trade shows over there. In many Asian cultures, status is very important. So that meant I had to go, as president of the company. Otherwise, we couldn't get the right people in the room for meetings." He paused. "Do you have any idea how long it takes to fly from Chicago to Hong Kong?"

"I haven't a clue."

"Long time."

"Is that why there's a bathroom in the jet."

"And why the seats turn into flat beds."

"Not to brag," she put in saucily. "But I went as far as Denver this year."

"You're lucky. If I could do all my work in Chicago, I'd never travel at all."

Mandy didn't like the idea of Caleb not traveling. The only way she'd ever see him in the future is if he traveled to Colorado. "The jet seemed pretty comfortable," she noted.

"So, you see my point."

"Your point being, why fly commercial when you can take your own Gulf Stream?"

"Okay, now that was definitely sarcastic."

"It was," she admitted with a grin.

He sobered. "It's funny. What looks like luxury and unbelievable convenience that ninety-nine percent of the population can't access, is really just me trying to survive." He set down his wineglass and shifted closer to her. "I don't know if I'm saying this right. But money and success aren't what you expect. The responsibility never goes away. You worry everyday. Literally thousands of people depend on your decisions, and you never know who's your friend, who's using you and who's out to get you. The risks are high. The stakes are high. And you go weeks on end without an opportunity to catch your breath, never mind relax."

Mandy thought she did understand. "Are you relaxed now?" she asked.

He nodded. "Amazingly, at this moment, yes."

"That's good."

"It's you."

It was her turn to toast him, keeping it light. "Happy to help out."

He tapped his fingers against his knee. "You know, I believe you're serious about that. It's one of the things I like best about you."

"I'm relaxing?" She wasn't sure whether to take that as a compliment or not. Relaxing could also be boring. And she couldn't possibly be anywhere near as exciting as the women he usually dated.

Dated. She paused. Was this a date?

"You're not thinking about what I can do for you," said Caleb. "You're sitting over there, looking off-the-charts gorgeous, enjoying a rather pedestrian wine, without a single complaint."

She glanced at her glass. "Should I be complaining? Do I have poor taste in wine?"

"I'm definitely not saying this right. You care about how I feel, about what you can do for me. Do you know how rare that is?"

"Do I really have bad taste in wine?"

Caleb laughed, picked up his glass, toasted her and drank the remainder. "It tastes perfectly fine to me." He stared softly at her for a long moment. "But I know you know what I mean."

She fought an impish grin, going with the impulse to keep joking. "I figure it's a toss up between you saying I'm boring and you saying I'm unsophisticated."

He deliberately set down his empty glass. Moved so he was right next to her and lifted her glass from her fingers. "You, Mandy, are anything but boring."

"But I am unsophisticated."

He opened his mouth, but she kept talking before he could say something that was complimentary but patently untrue. "I'm a ranch girl, Caleb. I've barely left the state. I haven't even seen my own sister at Liberty in New York."

Caleb blinked in obvious surprise. "You haven't seen Katrina dance?"

"Oh, I've seen her dance a few times, during the last years she was at college." Mandy thought back to the experiences. "She is incredible. But I haven't been to New York since she joined Liberty. I haven't seen her perform at the Emperor's Theatre as a principle dancer."

"You need to do that," he said decisively.

"I do. And maybe I should take in a wine-tasting class while I'm in the city. Clearly, my palate needs some work."

"Your palate is perfect." He kissed her. "Better than perfect." He kissed her again.

She responded immediately, arms going around his neck, hugging him close, returning the kiss with fervor, reveling in the feel of his strong body pressing itself up against hers.

"I'm taking you to New York," he whispered against her lips.

"Now?"

"Not now." His warm hand covered her knee, sliding up her bare thigh, beneath the red dress. "Right now, I'm hoping to take you someplace else entirely."

She smiled against his mouth. "I can hardly wait."

He drew back to look at her. "But after this, Mandy. Whatever happens with…" He seemed to search for words. "Whatever happens with all the stuff that's around us… Afterwards, I am taking you to New York. We're going to watch your sister perform, drink ridiculously expensive wine and stay in a hotel suite overlooking Central Park."

"Is that before or after you take me to Rio for a manicure?"

"Your choice."

His fingertips found the silk of her panties, and she groaned his name.

"Oh, Mandy," he breathed, kissing her deeply, lifting her into his arms.

He stood, striding toward the king-size bed, flicking the lights off as he passed each switch.

He set her on her feet next to the bed, threw back the covers, then gently urged her down, following her, stretching out, his gaze holding hers the entire time.

He gently stroked her cheek with the backs of his fingers, smoothed her hair, ran his fingertips along her collarbone, pushing down the straps of her dress. "I am so very glad you're here."

She kissed his mouth, ran her tongue over the seam of his lips, then opened wide and kissed him deeply and endlessly. "There's nowhere else I want to be."

He took it slow, gently and tenderly lingering over every inch of her skin with his kisses and caresses. Mandy had never felt so cherished. And when they were naked, and fused together, she curled her body around him, holding him tight, gasping as his slow deliberate strokes took her higher and higher.

Reality disappeared, and she clung almost desperately to lovemaking that went on and on. When she finally cried his name, they collapsed into each others arms. She was certain she'd ended up in Heaven.

Her heartbeat was deep and heavy. Her lungs worked overtime. And she inhaled Caleb's musky scent, clinging tightly to him, fighting sleep and willing the rest of the world away for just as long as possible.

Ten

The next day, Caleb couldn't seem to bring himself to let go of Mandy. He held her hand, occasionally pulled her sideways against him. She'd put up with it for a short time, but then she kept freeing herself, obviously not comfortable with the intimacy around her family. Caleb didn't care who saw them, as they wandered through the grounds of the Lyndon Regional Rodeo. It was opening day, and everyone agreed it was worth staying to watch.

The rodeo had always been a fun, lighthearted, family affair, and Caleb was astonished to see how much it had grown since he'd last attended. He'd rode bucking broncs that year. He was seventeen and too young to realize he was mortal.

He hadn't finished in the money. But Reed had won the trophy for steer wrestling. Cocky, reckless and in high spirits, they'd spent his five-hundred-dollar prize on beer and flashy new boots for both of them. Now, Caleb found himself wondering if those boots, barely worn, were still stored in his bedroom closet, and what Reed had done with his pair.

He and Mandy made their way through the midway, toward

the main arena. The announcer was pumping up the crowd for the first event. Children ran from ride to ride, shrieking with excitement, sticky cotton candy in their hands and balloon hats on their heads.

One young boy cried as his helium balloon floated away. Seth was quick to snag a wandering vendor and replace the balloon. They boy's mother was grateful, and Seth was sure to introduce himself by his full name.

"Hopefully, another vote," Abigail said to Mandy and Caleb in an undertone.

"He's very good at schmoozing," Caleb agreed. He had to admit, he admired Seth's easy manner with the crowds. He seemed to know everybody, and they seemed to respect him. Those he didn't know, he quickly met.

"Are we here for the rodeo or a campaign stop?" Mandy asked her sister. Abigail just laughed in response.

Caleb was dressed in blue jeans, boots and a white Western-style dress shirt. But it was all new, and he felt like a dandy, more than a little out of place among the working cowboys. He wondered how may people assumed he was a tourist. Certainly, all the competitors would peg him right off. He wished there was time to scuff up the boots and fade his jeans.

"Hey, Mandy," a woman called from behind them.

Mandy turned and so did Caleb, and her hand came loose from his.

The woman looked to be about thirty years old. She wore a pair of tight jeans, a battered Stetson hat and a wide, tooled leather belt. She was a bit thick around the middle, her hair was nondescript brown, and her red checked shirt was open to reveal a navy T-shirt beneath. She clearly belonged here at the rodeo.

"You riding today?" she asked Mandy.

Caleb looked at Mandy with curiosity. She competed in rodeo events?

"Not today," Mandy answered. "We just happened to be in town and thought we'd take it in."

"Heard about your dad," the woman continued, her expression switching to one of sympathy. "I was real sorry about that."

"Thank you," Mandy acknowledged. "We appreciate it. But he's doing very well, making more progress every day."

"Good to hear. Good to hear." Then the woman stuck out her hand to Caleb. "Lori Richland."

"Used to be Lori Parker," Mandy put in.

Caleb recognized the name. Lori had been a year behind him in high school. He didn't remember very much about her.

He accepted her hand. "Caleb Terrell."

"Woo hoo," she sang. "Wait till I tell Harvey I got a look at you." She gave Caleb's hand a playful tug, looking him up and down. "We heard you were back in town. Sorry to hear about your dad, too."

"Thank you," Caleb said simply.

Lori turned her attention to Mandy. "I've got Star Dock over at the stables if you want to enter the barrels."

"I hadn't planned—"

"Go for it," Lori insisted. "He loves competing." She looked back at Caleb. "The crowds and the applause does something for that horse."

"Hey, Abby," Lori called over Mandy's shoulder. "Steer undecorating?"

Abby approached them. "Yeah? If you've got a horse here, I'm game."

"Pincher's been doing really well lately. And tell your brothers to check with Clancy over at the pens. We need some good local competitors in team, steer roping."

Caleb had a sudden flashback to him and Reed practicing roping out on the range. They'd had plans to someday compete together, but Reed's big body made him a natural for steer wrestling, while Caleb had liked the adrenalin rush of the bucking horses.

Lori looked directly at Caleb. "What about you? What are you going to enter?"

Caleb held up his palms in mock surrender. "Not today."

He was not getting anywhere near anything that bucked. And he was completely out of practice for all of the events.

Mandy leaned over to Lori and spoke in a mock whisper. "He's been away in the big city. Riding a desk for a few years."

Lori checked him out up and down. "Doesn't look too soft."

"Why does everybody keep being surprised about that?" Caleb asked Mandy.

"Because it's true." She patted his shoulder consolingly. "You don't look too bad for a city slicker."

"You're too kind," he drawled.

"You should take it as a compliment," said Mandy.

"Maybe we'll throw you in the greased pig chase," Lori teased Caleb.

"Pass," said Caleb. "But you go right ahead and have a good time with that."

Lori tipped her head back and gave a throaty laugh.

"Barrels start in about an hour," she said to Mandy. "Better check the schedule for the rest." With a wave, she strode away into the crowd.

"You're going to compete?" Caleb asked.

"Sure," said Mandy. "I could win a thousand dollars."

"Don't want to pass up a chance like that." He found his gaze drifting to Travis and Seth. Abigail had obviously given them the news about the chance to enter the rodeo, and they now had their heads together talking strategy.

For a sharp second, Caleb missed Reed so badly, it brought a pain to the centre of his chest.

Then Mandy slipped her hand into his. She leaned in, and her tone went sultry. "You want to be my stable hand?"

He tugged her tight against his side. "I'll be anything you want me to be."

She grinned. "I'm holding you to that."

He kept her hand in his as they headed for the horse pens in the competitors area around back of the arena.

There, she quickly got down to business, signing up, paying

the entry fee and checking out the horse and tack Lori had offered her.

When she was ready to go, Caleb crossed to the competitors grandstand, where he could get a better view. He caught sight of the other Jacobs siblings in the distance, getting ready for their own events, and he had to struggle not to feel like the odd man out.

But once the barrel-racing event started, he got caught up with the cheering, coming to his feet when Mandy galloped into the arena. She made a very respectable run. Halfway through the competition, and she was in second place.

She joined him sitting in the stands for the last few competitors, leaning up against him as they laughed and cheered. She managed to hang on to third place until the last competitor knocked her to fourth, just out of the money.

Caleb gave her a conciliatory hug, telling her he was sorry.

But she shrugged philosophically. "Easy come, easy go."

"I'll spring for a corn dog if it'll make you feel better," he offered.

She turned up her nose. "What corn dog? I'm holding out for Rio."

He pretended to ponder for a moment. "I suppose I could do both."

"Truly?" She blinked ingenuously up at him.

"Yes," he told her sincerely. He realized in that moment he'd give her anything she wanted.

"You're a gentleman, Caleb Terrell," she cooed, threading her arm through his.

"And, dust notwithstanding—" he pretended to wipe a smudge off her cheek "—you, Mandy Jacobs, are a lady."

Her face was scrubbed clean of makeup today, and her hair was pulled back in a simple ponytail, but in the sunshine she looked just as beautiful as she had last night. He had trouble tearing his gaze away from her.

Her attention went to the ring. She cheered and gave a shrill whistle as the barrel-race winners received their awards in the middle of the arena.

"You just whistled." He laughed.

"Bet the girls back in Chicago don't do that."

"They don't eat corn dogs, either."

"Poor things. They don't know what they're missing."

The team roping had started. Caleb couldn't help but admire the talent of the cowboys and the rapt attention of well-bred horses. A few of the steers escaped, but most were swiftly roped and released by the cowboys.

"Here we go." Mandy leaned forward as her brothers lined up in the box. The steer was released, and the men sprang to action, horses hooves thundering, ropes spinning around their heads. Travis took the head, turned the spotted steer, and Seth quickly followed-up with the heels.

The horses stilled, and the flag waved. Their time was five point three seconds, causing Mandy to shout and punch a fist in the air. The time had put them in first place. They released their ropes and tipped their hats to the crowd, acknowledging the cheers.

They shook hands as they rode out of the arena, and Seth playfully knocked off Travis's hat. One of the clowns retrieved it for him, and the two disappeared from sight around the end of the fence.

Caleb felt another hitch in his chest. His reaction was silly. Even if he did meet his brother after all these years, it wasn't as if they'd be doing any team roping. Caleb was way too far out of practice. Besides, he was too old to come off a horse.

"Are you hungry?" Mandy asked.

"You don't seriously want a corn dog."

"I was thinking a funnel cake. Sprinkled with sugar, please."

"How on earth do you stay so slim?" Most of the women he knew in Chicago survived on leaf lettuce and bok choy.

"Exercise and clean living," she answered.

"So, you're serious?"

"I never joke about funnel cake."

Caleb shook his head in amazement, coming to his feet. "One funnel cake, coming up. You going to eat the whole thing, or will you share?"

"With you, I guess I could share."

He gave her a wink and made his way down the worn wooden benches, meeting Travis and Seth at the bottom.

"Nice." He nodded, shaking each of their hands in congratulations. He checked the board to find them still on top with six competitors left. "Looks like you might finish in the money."

"Seven-hundred and fifty bucks," Travis confirmed with a sharp nod. "That'll pay for the trip."

"I'm going on a funnel-cake run. Anyone interested?"

"Gads, no," said Seth. "I don't know how Mandy eats those things."

"She's got a sweet tooth," said Travis. His level gaze stayed on Caleb for a couple of beats.

Caleb raised his brows. If Travis had something to say, he might as well spit it out.

Seth glanced between the two men.

"You heard anything from Reed?" Travis asked, surprising Caleb.

The question triggered emotions that were close to the surface today, and it took him a second to recover. He shook his head. "Not a word."

"He still takes first in the steer wrestling every year," said Travis.

Caleb nodded his acknowledgment but didn't answer.

But Travis wasn't finished yet. "Mandy thinks you should talk to him before you sell the ranch."

The announcer's voice became more animated over the loudspeaker as the next team of ropers left the box, stirring up a cloud of dust.

"Mandy thinks a lot of things," said Caleb.

"I'm not sure she's wrong on this."

"Well, I can't talk to him if he's not here." Caleb made to leave.

"You can hold off on the sale," said Travis.

"You're selling?" asked Seth, an obvious note of incredulity in his voice. "Why on earth would you do that?"

"Yes," Caleb answered shortly, pivoting in the dust and starting to walk away.

"Whoa," Seth caught up to him, but Travis, at least, had the good grace to stay behind. "What gives?"

"What gives is that I'm not explaining myself to you and Travis in the middle of a rodeo crowd."

"Fair enough." Seth nodded easily, keeping pace. "But what about Reed? He get a say in this?"

"Reed left town, no forwarding address, no phone number."

"But how can you sell it without him?" Seth paused. "You know, I honestly thought he'd inherit the whole thing."

Caleb altered his course to angle toward the concession stands. "Well, he didn't. I did."

"Not the whole thing."

"Yes, the whole thing."

"But—"

"Haven't a clue," Caleb preempted the obvious question.

Seth's tone turned thoughtful. "And that's why Reed disappeared."

"I would think so." They came to the lineup and joined the end.

"Are you getting a funnel cake?" Caleb asked Seth.

"Just keeping you company."

"Not necessary."

But Seth didn't leave. After a few minutes of silence, he spoke up again. "Do you need the money?"

Caleb laughed darkly at that suggestion. "The money's Reed's. It's going to sit in a bank account until he shows his face."

"And the rush is?"

"Has it occurred to you that this is none of your business?"

"Absolutely."

"Then, go away."

"Has it occurred to you that I'm your friend?"

Caleb couldn't form an answer to that one. He liked and respected Seth, but he was beginning to feel as if he was surrounded by kind, well-meaning, meddlers, pushing him in a direction he didn't want to go.

"Seriously, Caleb. This is a huge decision."

"It's already listed."

"Unlist it."

"I don't want it," Caleb barked. "I don't need it. And Reed's better off without it." He glared at Seth, while the festival swirled around them, midway rides jangling, children shrieking and the rodeo announcements blaring in the distance.

After a long minute, Seth gave a curt nod of acquiescence. And Caleb turned to the teenager in the paper hat and placed his order.

Eleven

The trip to Lyndon and the rodeo day over and done with, Mandy and the local vet were working their way through a list of minor injuries and ailments in the ranch's horses. Mid-afternoon, they were inside the barn looking at a quarter-horse colt who'd been limping on and off for about a week. The colt's left fetlock felt warm, and Mandy was worried about infection.

"Mandy?" a whispered voice questioned from behind them, the person obviously being careful not to spook the colt.

Mandy smoothly rose from the colt's leg and turned to find Robby, one of the young hands, waiting.

"There's someone on the office phone for you," he told her quietly. "Danielle something? She's pretty insistent."

"I'll take it," Mandy agreed, optimism rising within her. "Can you give Dr. Peters a hand while I'm gone, Robby?" She dusted her hands off on her jeans and moved from the stall to the main barn aisle.

The young man set aside his manure fork and took Mandy's place in the stall.

Anticipation tightened Mandy's stomach as she paced her

way quickly to the small office that sat just inside the main door of the barn.

She closed the door behind her for privacy and picked up the phone. "Danielle?"

"Mandy?"

"It's me." Mandy forced herself to sit down on the leather chair with wheels, telling herself to stay calm. "You have news?"

"I do. Enrico found Reed."

Mandy's spirit soured. "Yes!" They'd found him. They'd finally found him. "Thank you."

"Right now, he's staying at a hotel in Helena."

"Really?" That information surprised Mandy. "Reed is in Montana?" She'd assumed he was at least still in Colorado.

"The Bearberry Inn. He's been there a couple of days, but there's no way of knowing how long he'll stay."

"Don't worry. I'm leaving right away." Mandy hopped up from the chair, cataloging exactly what she'd have to do to get to the airport, get to Helena and find Reed. When she did, she was cornering him and demanding to know what the heck he thought he was doing.

Okay, maybe she wouldn't demand. Maybe she'd just ask him. But, first, maybe she'd just hug him. After the past few weeks like he'd had, the man was going to need a hug.

"Call me when you get there," said Danielle. "And please, please convince him to come home. Whatever it takes."

"I will," Mandy promised.

"If we can wrap this up by Wednesday, my life gets a whole lot easier."

"Uh, okay." Two days. "I'll do my best." Mandy signed off.

As she headed across the yard, toward the house, she remembered the Brazilian deadline was looming. That was obviously the rush. Danielle was going to do everything in her power to get Caleb to Sao Paulo in time to deal with the banking regulators.

That meant there was every chance he'd be gone before

Mandy got back. As soon as Reed agreed to return, she'd have to call Danielle. Danielle would obviously call Caleb, and Caleb would have no reason to stay in Colorado, especially if his business depended on him getting to Brazil.

That meant the two brothers might not even see each other. They might not get a chance to talk. And once the crisis was over, things could easily go back to the status quo, Reed here, Caleb there, still estranged from each other.

Mandy trotted up the stairs, across the porch and into the ranch house foyer. Maybe keeping Danielle's search a secret from Caleb had been the wrong idea. Taking Caleb with her to Helena made much more sense. If he'd come, he'd have to talk to Reed. That would break the ice. And he'd still have time to make it to Brazil. And, afterward, maybe he'd come back.

She pulled off her boots in the front foyer and headed for the second floor, intending to have a quick shower and pack an overnight case.

She warmed to her modified plan. Reed was sure to be happy with Caleb's honor and generosity. The two brothers could talk in Helena, resolve things and then... Well, the plan got a little fuzzy after that, but at least it was a start.

She stripped of her shirt, peeled off her jeans, discarded her underwear and stepped into a hot shower.

She hadn't talked to Caleb since they'd returned from Lyndon last night after the rodeo. Seth and Travis had finished in second place, and after a celebratory beer and a round of burgers, she and Caleb had driven back together.

He'd been unusually quiet on the drive, but had kissed her good-night, and he'd told her he was going to miss her overnight. Nothing wrong with that. Everything was fine between them. She could safely broach the subject of Reed.

Perhaps she could do it between kisses. That would be manipulating the situation. But it was for a good cause.

Then again, that was probably a bad idea. She'd go with a straight-up outline of the facts. Caleb liked facts, and the facts were on her side in this.

She dressed, blow-dried her hair, put on a touch of makeup, a pair of clean jeans, a striped T-shirt and a navy blazer. Then she tossed a few clothes into the overnight bag, left a note to her brothers, saying she'd call them when she got to Helena, and jumped into a pickup truck.

The ride to the Terrell ranch took its usual twenty minutes, but it felt much longer. She pulled up to the house, took a very deep, bracing breath and set out to reason with Caleb.

When she knocked, he called out a huffed "come in."

"Caleb?" she called back as the door opened. She could hear scraping sounds coming from the living room.

She followed the noise, rounding the corner from the foyer to find him surrounded by cardboard packing boxes, a tape dispenser in his hand, as he sealed one of them up.

"What are you doing?" Her tone came out sharper than she'd intended.

"Packing." He voiced the obvious.

"But, why?" What had happened? Had she missed something? Had he already sold the ranch?

"Mostly, because it's not going to pack itself," he answered.

"But I thought—"

"Can you hand me another box?"

Mandy was too stunned to move. She felt sick to her stomach.

"Did you sell?" she managed on a harsh whisper.

"Not yet."

She put out a hand to brace herself against the back of the sofa, all but staggering in relief. There was still time.

"A box?" he asked again.

"Sure." She picked up a flattened box from a pile beside her feet and handed it over. She met his gaze. "And, if we find Reed?"

His jaw tensed. "Seriously, Mandy. I'm not having that conversation all over again."

She swallowed against her dry throat. "But, if we did find him. Like, right away. Would you be willing—"

He smacked the box on the coffee table in the middle of the room, startling her. The thread of anger in his voice was crystal clear. "What is *with* you people? This isn't a Jacobs family decision. It's my decision."

His tone set her back. "But—"

"No." He jabbed his finger in her direction. "No, Mandy. I am packing. I am selling. I am going to Brazil and then back to Chicago. And I'm not changing my mind. You won't change it. Seth won't change it. And neither will Travis."

So much for gentle. So much for reasonable. "You're a stubborn fool."

"You're not the first one to notice."

She came around the end of the pile of boxes, staring straight into his eyes, lowering her voice. "You step over this cliff, Caleb, and we can't come back."

He went still for a very long moment, staring levelly back. "We, as in you and me?"

"As in your brother, your family, your heritage."

"I can live with that." It was obvious he was serious, completely serious. There was no way she'd get him to Helena.

Though she told herself it was a much less significant matter, she couldn't seem to stop herself from asking. "What about me and you?"

His expression didn't change. He leaned in and gave her a fleeting kiss. It wasn't exactly a cold kiss, but it didn't invite anything further. "Me and you are still going to Rio."

She tried not to let his words hurt her, but they did. So her voice was laced with sarcasm when she answered. "Is that an 'I'll call you sometime, babe'?"

"That's not what I said."

She bit her tongue. He was right. He'd been up front and honest all along the way. All he'd ever offered was Rio and New York City. If it wasn't enough for her, she should have spoken up a long time ago.

She knew she couldn't change Caleb. But she could still help Reed. Pretending everything was fine, she stretched up and kissed Caleb on the cheek. "Rio sounds good. I gotta go. The vet's working with the horses today, and he's, well, they'll need me down there."

"Sure," Caleb agreed, flipping the box over to reinforce the bottom with a strip of tape. "See you later."

"Later," she echoed, turning to leave.

Caleb worked for about an hour, reassuring himself he was doing exactly the right thing. He couldn't stay here. He growing frighteningly attached to Mandy, and it got worse every day.

But every time he turned around in this house, there was another picture, another memento, another annoying memory trigger, like the woodsy scent of the throw blanket his mother had knit for the back of the sofa.

It had taken a long time for Chicago to feel like home, and he wasn't about to lose that. Not for the sake of his family's land, and not to be near Mandy for a few more days.

Mandy. He blew out a breath. He hadn't wanted to fight with her. But she had to understand. There was no hope that he'd erase his childhood, nor would he ever come to terms with it. The best he could hope for was to leave it far, far behind. So he didn't have to think about it every day of his life.

Still, he shouldn't have taken it out on her.

She was entitled to her opinion. And she held that particular opinion only because she was a compassionate, generous, caring person. She couldn't stand to see anyone hurt or upset, and that included Reed. And what did she get from Caleb for her trouble? Anger and the cold shoulder.

He needed to apologize.

Silently acknowledging he'd been a jerk, he deserted the packing job and headed for his SUV. He rammed it into Drive and peeled out.

Down the ranch roadway, he took the corners fast, his back tires breaking loose on the gravel ranch road. Then he sped along the main valley road to the arched gateway to the Jacobses' ranch. It was five minutes up the driveway, and then he was pulling up front of the house.

He knocked once, then let himself in to find Travis and Seth at the table, digging into steaks.

He glanced around. "Is Mandy upstairs?"

Seth shook his head. "You didn't talk to her before she left?"

"Left?"

Mandy sure hadn't said anything to Caleb about leaving.

"For Helena," said Travis. "I thought you must have gone with her, taken your jet."

Caleb walked farther into the room, his hands going to his hips. "She didn't say anything to me."

Seth glanced at his watch. "She said she'd call us when she landed at the airport. You hungry?"

No, Caleb wasn't hungry.

Mandy was gone. She'd left after their fight. What did that mean? Was she going to pull the same stunt as Reed and disappear when things didn't go her way?

What the hell was the matter with her?

He struggled to keep the anger from his voice. "Did she say where she was going in Helena?"

"Nope," said Travis, obviously unconcerned. Sure, *now* he didn't worry about his sister.

"Do you have any business interests there, suppliers?" Caleb pressed.

"Nothing," said Seth.

"She did have a college friend who was from there," Travis offered. "I don't know her name or anything."

"But it was a woman?"

Seth gave him a confused look.

Travis scoffed out an amused laugh.

Caleb headed for the door. "If you hear anything, send me a text."

"Will do," said Travis.

"Where you going?" Seth called out behind him.

"Helena," Caleb answered. "Let me know if you hear from Mandy."

"What on earth is going—" Seth's voice abruptly disappeared as Caleb shut the front door.

Caleb stomped his way back to the SUV. It seemed impossible that Mandy had a sudden desire to visit an old friend. Unless the old friend was in trouble. But, if that was the case, she should have told him. He could have lent her his jet to get to Helena.

Unless it was Mandy going to see her old friend for solace. Could she be that angry with him? She'd said yes to Rio. That was a good sign, right?

He started the vehicle and pulled it into gear, wheeling through the roundabout and back out the driveway. He reached for his phone and dialed her cell with his thumb.

He got voice mail, and didn't really care to leave a message.

By the time he hit the main road, his confusion had turned to anger. No matter what her reason for leaving, the least she could have done was call him, or send him a text if she was too mad for a civil conversation. She'd let her brothers know where she was headed. Well, at least the rudimentary details. A motel name would have been nice.

Coming up on the highway, he dialed the pilot. It would be late before he got to Lyndon, but the airport was equipped for after-dark takeoffs, and they could land in Helena on instruments.

Having managed to get a flight from Lyndon to Denver last night, then a flight into Helena this morning, Mandy had camped out in the restaurant of the Bearberry Inn for over two hours. It was three in the afternoon, but there was still no sign of Reed.

The front desk had refused to give out his room number, and she didn't want to call him, for fear he'd refuse to see her. She'd chosen a table in a back corner where she could watch both the restaurant and the front desk across the lobby without being easily seen.

She figured her last hope was to get him to come back to Lyndon Valley right away. If she did it quickly, there was a chance Caleb would still be there. If not, she was certain he'd finish packing and leave for Sao Paulo, sale or no sale. But if she could make it in time, Caleb, the stubborn fool, would be forced to have a conversation with his brother.

Just as Mandy was ordering her third cup of coffee, her patience was rewarded. She caught a glimpse of Reed's profile, his tall, sturdy frame, striding across the lobby toward the bank of elevators. Quickly canceling her order, she tossed some money on the table and jumped up, grabbing her shoulder bag and slinging it over her blazer.

She trotted out of the restaurant, determined to catch him. A few feet away, she called out his name.

He turned and stared at her in obvious shock.

"Mandy?" He glanced around the expansive lobby. "What on earth are you doing here?"

"I'm looking for you." She immediately hugged him, and he hugged her back. But her joy at finding him turned almost instantly to frustration. Drawing back, she socked him in the shoulder. "What is the matter with you?"

"Me? I'm not the one who appeared out of nowhere."

"Do you have any idea how worried I've been?"

A couple of guests gave them curious glances as they walked past, causing Reed to take Mandy's arm and lead her toward a glass door that led to the hotel courtyard.

"Why would you worry?" he asked. "What are you doing in Helena? How on earth did you know I was here?"

They made it outside to the relative privacy of an interior courtyard with a table-dotted patio, a manicured, green lawn, towering trees and colorful, raised brick gardens.

"I didn't know if you'd been kidnapped, shanghaied, injured, arrested or mugged."

"Kidnapped? You've got to be kidding me. Like somebody's going to hold me for ransom."

"You know what I mean."

"I'm fine. Nobody's going to mug me, Mandy. At night, on the darkened streets? *I'm* the guy people are afraid of."

"I can't believe you didn't call me."

"I can't believe you were worried."

"Why didn't you at least send me a text?"

"Because I didn't want anyone to know where I was."

She jabbed her thumb against her chest, voice going up. "*I'm* not anyone."

"You'd have told your brothers."

"I would not."

He gave her a look of disbelief.

Okay, maybe she would have, if they'd asked. She wasn't the world's best liar.

He glanced around the courtyard. "Do you want to sit down?"

"Sure," she agreed, taking a deep breath. She'd found him. Whatever else happened, at least she'd found him.

He guided her to one of the small tables, pulling out her chair before taking the seat across from her. "You shouldn't have come."

Okay. Now was the time to tread carefully. She had to make Reed want to come back to the ranch and be willing to speak to Caleb. Otherwise, she'd never get him to budge.

She struggled with where to start.

"Mandy?" he prompted.

"Why Helena?" she asked, giving him a smile, intending to ease her way in, telling herself to relax and act as though everything was normal.

"Besides the fishing? It's good ranch country, Mandy. I've had a job offer here."

"Of course you've had a job offer. You could probably have a thousand job offers if you wanted them."

He allowed himself a smile. "You're such an optimist."

"I am," she agreed. "And I have faith in you. You're an amazing person, Reed, a phenomenal person—"

"You know, don't you?"

She played dumb. "Know what?"

"About the will." He waited.

"Fine," she conceded. "I know about the will."

"How?"

She straightened in her chair, leaning over the round metal-framed, glass-topped table. "Can I start by saying I understand that you're upset."

"You can if you want. But that doesn't tell me anything. And it only puts off whatever it is you're dancing around here."

"It was a mistake to leave, Reed."

He scoffed out a laugh.

"You don't understand what's going—"

"How do you know about the will?"

"I want you to come back."

"You do, do you?"

"I do."

"You don't know what you're asking."

She reached across the table for his big hand. "I know exactly what I'm asking. If you'll just—"

"How did you find out about the will, Mandy?"

She closed her eyes for a brief second. "Fine. Caleb told me."

Reed gave a snort of derision, pulling his hand back. "Didn't take him long."

"Didn't take me long at all," came another deep, masculine voice.

Mandy's heart all but stopped.

She turned her head. "Caleb," she breathed.

"Was this stunt part of some grand plan?" he asked her, not even acknowledging his brother.

Reed came to his feet.

"I found Reed," she stated the unnecessary. "That's what I wanted to tell you—"

"You hoped I'd follow you?" Caleb demanded.

She was confused by his statement. "Follow—"

He gave a cold laugh. "Of course you knew I'd follow you. How could I not follow you?"

"What?" she couldn't help asking, giving a small shake of her head. If she'd wanted him to follow her, she'd have told him where she was going.

"That's what this was all about, all along." His blue gaze crackled into hers. "You realized you couldn't get me to talk to him by being honest."

What? No. Wait a minute.

Reed stepped forward. "Nobody invited you to join us."

Mandy whirled her gaze. "Reed, no. Let him explain."

Caleb sized up his brother. "What the hell is the matter with you?"

Reed's voice was stone cold. "Somebody stole my ranch."

"You didn't stay to defend it."

"Right. Like I'm going to hang around under those circumstances."

"You hung in there with Wilton."

Reed clenched his jaw down tight, and the edges of his mouth turned white. "Shut up."

"I don't think I will."

Mandy was starting to panic. She stepped between the two angry men. "Reed. Listen to me. He's giving it back. Caleb's giving you back the ranch."

"I'm selling the ranch," Caleb countered.

She ignored him and continued talking to Reed, her words spilling out fast. "That's how I found out about the will. Caleb came to Colorado to give it back to you."

"It doesn't matter," said Reed.

"How can it not matter?" she practically wailed.

"I don't want it," he spat.

"That's ridiculous," said Mandy. Her gaze took in both of them. "Come on, you two, quit being such—"

"You heard him," said Caleb.

She rounded on Caleb. "Of *course* he wants it back."

"Are you reading his mind?"

"I'm using logic and reason." Her expression of frustration took in both of them. "Something that seems to be in ridiculously short supply in this conversation."

Caleb angled his body toward Mandy, arms still by his sides, hands curled into fists. "You heard him. He said no."

"He'll change his mind."

"No, he won't." Caleb's gaze flicked to Reed. "He's as stubborn as a mule."

"At least I don't cut and run," Reed returned.

Caleb glared at his brother. "Back off."

"That's your specialty," said Reed. "And it's exactly what you're doing right now."

"I'm getting rid of an albatross that's been around our necks our entire lives."

"Around your neck?" Reed countered, squaring his shoulders, voice getting louder. "*Your* neck."

Caleb ignored the outburst. "I'll send you a check."

"Don't bother."

Mandy's stomach had turned to churning concrete. "Please, don't fight."

"Quit it," Caleb told her.

"Don't you yell at Mandy." Reed inched closer to his brother, shoulders squared, eyes hard as flints.

For a horrible moment, she thought they might come to blows.

"I'm not yelling at Mandy." When Caleb glanced back down at her, his expression had softened. "I'm not angry with you, Mandy. I swear I'm not. But you have your answer. He doesn't want the ranch."

"He does," she put in weakly.

"Are you ready to go home now?" Caleb asked.

Mandy shook her head. "I'm not going home. I just got here. Reed and I haven't even had a chance to—"

Caleb's voice went dark again, suspicion clouding his eyes. "To what?"

For a second, she thought she must have misunderstood. But his expression was transparent as usual. He actually thought there was something between her and Reed.

Mandy threw up her hands. "You can't possibly think that."

After all they'd been through? Could Caleb honestly think that? He'd asked her three times, and she'd told him over and over that they were just friends.

"So, you're staying here with him?" Caleb pressed.

She mustered her courage. Fine. If he wanted to think that, let him think that. "Yes, I am. I'm staying here with Reed."

Caleb's voice went quiet. "Is that what this was all about?"

She didn't understand the question.

"All along? Your plan was to make me like you, worm your way in until I can't—"

"Are you *kidding me?*" she all but shouted.

Did he seriously think she'd sleep with him to get him to stay? To not sell the ranch? Had he gone stark, raving mad?

He stared at her for a long minute. "Then, prove it. Prove you were being honest about your feelings all along."

What was he asking?

"Him or me, Mandy. What's it going to be?"

She froze.

Caleb couldn't ask this of her. She wasn't leaving Reed. If she did, Reed would disappear, and this time they wouldn't find him.

"So, it's him." Caleb's voice was completely devoid of emotion.

She hated his expression, hated his tone, hated that he was putting her in this impossible position. Under these circumstances, there was only one answer.

"Yes," she ground out. "It's him."

Caleb was silent, the breeze wafting, birds chirping in the trees, faint traffic noise from the other side of the building.

Finally, he gave her a curt nod, turned abruptly and stomped back into the hotel lobby.

She and Reed said nothing, simply staring at each other.

"I didn't mean for it to go this way," Mandy offered in a small voice, trying desperately not to picture Caleb getting in a cab or maybe a rental car in front of the hotel, making his way back to the airport, flying to Lyndon, packing up the ranch, maybe meeting with another buyer and never seeing her again.

Reed sat back down at the table, his expression implacable. "Did you honestly think putting yourself in the middle would help?"

Her chest tightened, and her throat started to close. "I..." She was at a loss for words. She'd thought it would help. She'd hoped it would help.

"Mandy, all you did was give us something more to fight about." Reed's words pierced her heart.

"I didn't mean..." She'd thought it would work. She'd honestly thought once they saw each other, they'd realize they were still brothers, that they still loved each other, and they'd reconcile.

But now she was in the middle, and Caleb was furious with her. He thought there was actually a chance that she was romantically interested in Reed. And he was gone. Likely gone for good.

Her voice began to shake. "I was only trying to help."

Reed nodded, and his fingers drummed on the glass top of the table. "I know. You can't help being you."

She drew back in confusion.

His expression eased. "We should get you a cape and a mask, Mandy. Swooping in, solving the problems of the world."

"I'm not..." But then Abigail's words came back to haunt her. Was this what she'd tried to warn Mandy about? *Was* Mandy substituting Reed for her own family? *Had* she become way too invested in Reed and Caleb's relationship?

Had she made a colossal mistake that was going to hurt them all?

Reed's dark eyes watched her closely while she struggled to bring her emotions back under control.

"Mandy?" he asked softly, a sad, ghost of a smile growing on his face. "How long have you been in love with Caleb?"

Mandy's stomach dove into a freefall. *"What?"* she rasped. "I didn't… I'm not… It isn't…" She could feel her face heat to flaming.

Reed cocked his head and waited.

She couldn't explain.

She wouldn't explain.

She didn't have to explain.

"I only slept with him," she blurted out.

Reed's lips formed a silent whistle. "And you just forced him to walk away and leave you with me? Oh, Mandy."

"I'm not in love with him," she managed. Falling in love with Caleb would be the most foolish move in the world. "It was a fling, a lark. It was nothing."

Reed reached across the table and took her hand in his. It was big, strong, callused. "You shouldn't have come here."

"I know that now," she admitted. She should have listened to her big sister. She should have minded her own business. Maybe if she had, Reed and Caleb would have found their way back without her.

"Go to the airport," Reed advised. "Go to Caleb right now."

But Mandy vigorously shook her head.

It was far too late for her to go to Caleb. And it wasn't what Reed thought. Caleb never offered her anything more than a plan for a fling in Rio. And even that was over now. She was pushing Caleb right out of her heart. Forever.

Twelve

Caleb's jet took off from the Sao Paulo airport, heading northwest into clear skies. The past two days had been an exercise in frustration, but with Danielle's help, he'd defeated the Brazilian banking system's red tape, and they were ready to start shipping raw materials next week.

They had a plant manager in place who spoke very good English. Their accounting and computer systems were set up, and they'd approved the hiring of three foremen who were now looking for local skilled trade workers.

"I'm going to set up a meeting with Sales and Accounting for Friday," said Danielle, punching a message into her PDA. "We have to watch the gross sales ceiling for the first six months, and I want everybody to understand the parameters."

"I'm not sure about Friday," said Caleb. He had to give final instructions to the moving company. The sooner the better as far as he was concerned.

"Why not?"

"I need to go to Colorado."

She whirled her head in his direction. "Wait a minute. *What?*"

"The outstanding water rights issue is playing havoc with property values, but I told the broker to take any deal. I want this done."

"But, your brother."

"What about my brother?"

"We found him. He's back. Sign the damn thing over to him and forget about it."

Caleb wasn't sure he'd heard right. "What do you mean *we* found him?"

Danielle straightened, her tone completely unapologetic. "Mandy wasn't going to get anywhere on her own, so I had Enrico make a few calls."

"Enrico found Reed?"

"Yes."

"And you didn't think you should run this by me?"

"I didn't charge you anything. Besides, you were off in la la land, reconnecting with your roots and ignoring your own best interests."

Caleb coughed and shifted in his airplane seat. "Okay, setting aside for a second that you went behind my back, Reed doesn't want the ranch. He turned it down."

"So? Put it in his name, anyway. I can have something drafted by the time we land in Chicago."

"I'm selling it," Caleb stated flatly, his frustration growing by the second.

"That's a ridiculous waste of your time. We need you in your office, with your head in the game, not out on the range, chasing—"

"Since when is my life managed by consensus?"

"Since you stopped managing it for yourself."

"I take a couple of weeks, a couple of weeks to visit my hometown."

"Since when could you care less about your hometown?"

Caleb didn't care about his hometown. Okay, maybe he did.

A little. It was fun hanging out with Travis again. And Seth was a great guy. And Mandy. He sucked in a breath. Mandy was going to be impossible to forget.

He'd tried to tell himself she'd lied about her feelings for him. But then he'd been forced to admit, she was. He'd been an absolute ass to accuse her of sleeping with him to get him to give Reed back the ranch. She'd never do that.

He'd even tossed the idea of seeing her again back and forth in his brain about a thousand times. Assuming that she'd be willing.

"Is it Mandy?" Danielle asked, startling him from his thoughts.

"Mandy what?"

"Are you going back to see Mandy?"

Caleb pressed his head hard against the high-backed seat. He had no idea how to answer that question. Mandy and the ranch were two completely different issues, but somehow they'd gotten all tangled up into one.

"If you've got a thing for her, you might as well go get it over with."

Caleb didn't have a thing for Mandy. Okay, well, he definitely had a thing for her. But the way Danielle put it, it sounded so crass. "How is this any of your business?"

"It's not. But we have this lawyer-client confidentiality thing going on, so I feel like I can be honest."

"Go be honest with someone else."

"Caleb." Her voice took on a tone of exaggerated patience, and she folded her hands in her lap. "We agreed that the solution was to give your brother back the ranch. I've handed it to you on a silver platter. You need to take it."

"I'm selling it," he repeated. He held the trump card, because there was nothing she could do to change his mind.

"Why?"

"Because he doesn't want it, and he's better off without it."

"So, you're doing this for him."

"Right."

"Yet, you haven't spoken to him in ten years."

"I spoke to him the other day." And it had been a surreal experience.

The person he'd fought with in Helena had been Reed, only not Reed. The new Reed was a twenty-seven-year-old man, broader and stronger than he'd been as a teenager, self-confident, self-assured. Part of Caleb had wanted to sit down and talk things over with him. And part of Caleb had wanted to throw Mandy over his shoulder and carry her away.

Mandy had said they were just friends. Yet, she stayed behind with Reed.

No, Caleb wasn't going to go there. Mandy told him she wasn't romantically involved with Reed, and he was going to believe her. The remaining question was whether she was interested in being romantically involved with Caleb.

Three days ago, he might have said maybe. Today, he'd definitely say no. But what if he went back? What if he treated her properly this time? Was there a chance of something between them?

He'd regretted walking away from her the second his feet hit the pavement in Helena. And he'd regretted it every minute since.

"I'm going to Colorado," he told Danielle with determination.

She shook her head and leaned back in her seat. "I can't save you from yourself, Caleb."

Sitting at his office desk, hitting send on a final email before he headed to the Chicago airport, Caleb heard someone enter through the open door.

He didn't look up. "Tell the driver I'll be ten more minutes."

"You have a driver?" came a deep, male voice.

Caleb turned sharply, swiveling his high-backed, leather chair to face the doorway.

Reed's large frame nearly filled the entrance. His boots added an inch to his six-foot-three-inch frame, and his midnight-black, Western-cut shirt stretched across his broad shoulders. In the office, he looked even more imposing than he had outside the hotel.

Caleb instantly came to his feet.

Reed didn't look angry, exactly. But he didn't look happy, either.

"What are you doing in Chicago?" was the only thing Caleb could think to say. He couldn't help but wonder if Mandy was with him.

"Wanted to talk to you," said Reed, taking a few paces into the office.

"Okay," Caleb offered warily. He'd been feeling off-kilter since he last saw Mandy, and his emotions continued to do crazy things to his logic. He really wasn't in the mood for a fight.

Reed stepped up to the desk. "Don't sell the ranch."

Caleb's jaw went lax.

"It's mine," said Reed.

Caleb didn't disagree with that. Morally and ethically, the ranch belonged to Reed.

"And I want it," Reed finished.

"You want it?" Something akin to joy came to life inside Caleb. Which was silly. The ranch wasn't good for Reed.

"Yes."

"Just like that." Caleb snapped his fingers.

Reed's dark eyes went hard. "No. Not just like that. Just like ten years of sweat and blood and hell."

"I was going to give you the money."

"I don't want the money. I want the land. My land. Our mother's land."

Caleb's heart gave an involuntary squeeze inside his chest.

"Did you forget her great-grandmother was born at Rock Creek?" asked Reed, voice crackling hard. "In that tiny falling-down house next to the waterfall?"

Of course Caleb hadn't forgotten. His mother had told them that story a hundred times.

"And her grandfather, her father. They're all buried on the hill, Caleb. You going to sell off our ancestors' bones?"

"You going to live with the memory of *him?*" Caleb blurted out.

"You going to let him defeat us?" Reed squared his shoulders. "He was who he was, Caleb."

"He killed her."

"I know. Do you think I don't know? And I can't bring her back." Reed's voice was shaking with emotion. "But do you know what I can do? What I'm going to do?"

Caleb was too stunned by the stark pain on his brother's face to even attempt an answer.

"I'm going to have her grandchildren. I'm going to find a nice girl, who loves Lyndon Valley, and I'm going to give her babies, and my first daughter will be named Sasha, and she will be loved, and she will be happy, and I will never, ever, *ever* let anyone hurt her."

Caleb's chest nearly caved in, while his heart stood still.

"Are you going to stand in my way?" Reed demanded, bringing his fist down on the desktop.

"No," Caleb managed through a dry throat.

"Good." Reed abruptly sat down and leaned back, crossing one boot over the opposite knee.

Caleb slumped in his chair. "Why didn't you say all that in the first place?"

"I've said it now."

"You're going to find a nice girl?" Caleb couldn't help but ask.

Reed nodded. "I am. A ranch girl. Someone like Mandy."

Caleb's spine went stiff, and his hands curled into fists.

Reed chuckled, obviously observing the involuntary reaction. "But not Mandy. Mandy's yours."

"No, she's not."

"Yeah. She is." Reed's tone was gruff, his eyes watchful. "Unless you're going to cut and run on her, too."

"I've never—"

"She's in love with you, Caleb. Not that you deserve her."

Reed had it all wrong.

"No, she's not. She's…" Caleb wasn't sure how to describe it. "Well, ticked off at me for one thing."

"Because you were such a jerk in Helena?"

"So were you."

Reed shrugged. "She'll forgive me in the blink of an eye, once I tell her I'm moving back."

"I'll sign it over to you today," Caleb offered. Now that the decision was made, he felt as if a weight had been lifted from his shoulders.

"What about Mandy?"

"That's between me and Mandy."

Caleb's brain was going off in about a million directions. Was it possible that she loved him? Had she told Reed she loved him? What business did she have loving him? She was a Lyndon Valley woman, and he was a Chicago man. How was that going to work?

"You slept with her, right?"

"None of your damn business."

"Do you think a woman like Mandy would sleep with just anyone?"

Of course Caleb didn't think she'd do that. And he couldn't help remembering how it felt to have her sleeping in his arms, the taste of her lips, the satin of her skin. And he wanted to feel it all again, so very, very badly.

"I thought you were going to take my head off in Helena." Reed chuckled low. "She had no idea what she did, by the way, telling you she was staying with me."

Caleb remembered that moment, when she had a choice and she hadn't picked him. He never wanted to feel that gut-wrenching anguish again. Mandy belonged with him. Not with Reed and not with any other man. Him, and him alone.

"You should go talk to her," Reed suggested.

"I *was* going to talk to her. Good grief, can I make at least one decision on my own?"

"Apparently not a good one. When were you going?"

Caleb pasted Reed with a mulish glare. "The jet's warming up on the tarmac."

"You have a jet?"

"Yes."

"Bring a ring."

Caleb drew back. "Excuse me?"

"You better bring a ring. You've been a jerk, and you need to apologize so she'll forgive you. And that whole thing's going to go a whole lot smoother with you on one knee."

"You haven't spoken to me in ten years, and you come back and the first thing you do is tell me who I should marry?"

"Second thing, technically," said Reed.

"Where do you get your nerve?"

"I'm bigger than you. I'm stronger than you. And it's not me who wants you to propose."

Caleb scoffed out a laugh at that. "It's not?"

"No. It's you."

Caleb stared at Reed, suddenly seeing past everything to the brother that he'd loved, still loved. Because, despite everything that had happened between them, it was still the same Reed. And he was still smart and, in this case, he was also right.

Caleb grinned. "You want to catch a ride back to Lyndon?"

Mandy had sworn to herself she wouldn't wallow in self-pity. She wouldn't pine away for Caleb, and she wouldn't let herself get involved any further in the brothers' conflict. She was going cold turkey.

Abigail was right. It was none of Mandy's business. They were grown men, and she had to let it go and let them work it out for themselves. Or not.

When it came down to it, Travis was right, too. Getting involved with Caleb had brought her nothing but heartache. What had she been thinking? That she could spend days and nights with a smart, compelling, exciting, successful man, and her heart wouldn't become involved.

She ran a curry comb over Ryder's haunch, dragging the dust out of the gelding's coat.

It was ironic, really. She'd spent the better part of her life giving advice out to people. She could be quite obnoxiously meddlesome at times. But she was always so certain she was right. She harped on people to take her advice, since she usually had some distance from the problem and a better perspective than the person who was in the thick of it. Yet, when people who loved her gave her perfectly reasonable, logical, realistic advice, she blew them off and did it her own way.

It served her right.

And she was now exactly where she deserved to be, losing Reed as her dear friend and neighbor and desperately missing Caleb. Reed had been right. She loved Caleb. She was madly, desperately in love with a man who'd never again give her the time of day.

If she closed her eyes, she could still feel his arms around her.

"Mandy?" his voice was so real, it startled her.

Her eyes flew open, and she blinked in complete astonishment. "Caleb?"

How could he be standing in her barn?

But he was.

She blinked again.

He *was.*

"Hello, Mandy." His tone was gentle. He was wearing a pair of worn blue jeans and a soft flannel shirt, looking completely at home as he slowly walked toward her.

She gripped the top rail of the stall with her leather-gloved hand. "What are you doing here?" she managed.

A slow smile grew on his face as he drew closer under the bright, hanging fluorescent lights. "You want to go to Rio?"

She watched his expression closely. "Is that a joke?"

"I'm completely serious."

"No. I am not going to Rio with you." She meant what she said. She was completely done with the Terrells.

He came to a halt a few feet away from her. "You said you would."

"That was before."

"Before what?"

Before her plan to fix everything had crashed and burned around her ears. Before she'd learned the truth about herself. Before she'd fallen in love with him and opened herself up to a world of hurt.

"Before we fought," she said instead.

"We didn't fight."

She shot him with a look of disbelief.

"Okay," he agreed. "We fought. And I'm sorry. I know you were just trying to help."

She shook her head, rubbing her palms across her cheeks and into her hair, trying to erase the memories. "I meddle. I know I meddle. And *I'm* the one who's sorry."

"I forgive you. Now, come to Rio."

"No."

"Come to Rio and marry me."

"N— *What?*"

"I thought…" He moved slowly closer, carefully, as if he was afraid to spook her. "I thought we could fly to Rio, get a manicure, have a blender drink and you could marry me."

There was a roaring inside her brain while she tried to make sense of his words. "Caleb, what are you trying to—"

He reached out and took her hands. "I'm trying to say that I love you, Mandy. And I like it when you meddle. I especially like it when you meddle with me."

Her heart paused, then thudded forcefully back to life, singing through her chest.

He loved her? He *loved* her?

Exhilaration burst through her.

She let out an involuntary squeal and launched herself into his arms. He hugged her tight, lifting her off the ground and spinning her around.

"Why? How?" she couldn't help but ask, voice muffled in the crook of his neck. She didn't expect this, didn't deserve this.

"I don't know why, but how? Mostly I just think about how beautiful you are, how sexy you are, how smart and caring and funny." He drew back and kissed her mouth. His lips were warm, soft, delicious and tender.

When he finally drew back and lowered her to her feet, she gazed up into his eyes. "I love you, too, Caleb. So very much."

"So, you'll come to Rio?"

"You know my family won't let you marry me in Rio."

"They can come along. I have a pretty big plane."

"We have to wait until my dad gets better."

"Of course we do," he agreed, kissing her all over again.

He captured both of her hands in his. His blue eyes danced under the lights. "You by any chance interested in a ring?" he asked.

She swallowed, unable to find her voice.

He tapped his shirt pocket, and she made out a telltale square bulge.

Joy flooded her. "You brought a ring to this engagement?"

"I did. A diamond."

Her lips broke into a grin. "Let's see it."

He reached into his pocket and extracted a small, white leather box. "It was Reed's idea."

"You talked to Reed?"

"He's inside with your brothers."

"Reed is *here?*" She couldn't believe it.

"Any chance we can focus on the ring right now?" Caleb popped open the spring-loaded top.

A beautiful, square-cut diamond solitaire in yellow gold was nestled against deep purple velvet. The sight took her breath away.

He leaned in and spoke in a husky whisper. "Do I know how to do a proposal or what?"

"That's one gorgeous ring."

"You like it?"

"I love it."

"Because we can exchange it if you want."

"Are you kidding? What else could I possibly want in a ring?"

Using his blunt fingers, he extracted it from the box.

She held out her left hand, and he smoothly pushed it onto her ring finger. It fit. She held her hand at arms length, flexing her wrist and watching the sparkle.

"This should shut Travis up," she mused.

"Yes." Caleb kissed her finger with the ring. "Because that was my secret plan. I figured, you know, if you'd marry me, it would be a bonus. But what I was really looking to do was get your brother off my back."

"We're really going to do this? You and me? Us?" Both her brain and her emotions were operating on overload. Caleb had come back to Lyndon Valley. He loved her. They were staying together. It defied imagination.

"Just as soon as you'll let me."

Uncertainty suddenly overtook her. "But, what then? Where do we go? Where do we live? My family's here. You're there."

"Well, Reed will be back living at his ranch."

She froze. "Seriously?"

Caleb nodded.

"He's coming home?"

"He's already home."

She hugged Caleb tight, and his arms went fully around her. "Part time here," he said. "Part time in Chicago. We made it work for two weeks. I'm sure we can make it work for the rest of our lives."

Mandy sighed and burrowed herself in his chest. "For the rest of our lives."

Once again, Caleb couldn't seem to bring himself to let go of Mandy.

Back inside the ranch house, her brothers, Abigail and Reed all gathered around them, admiring her ring, hugging and kissing and laughing their congratulations. When they eventually gave way, Abigail went to the kitchen to find a bottle of champagne.

Caleb lowered himself into a leather armchair, and drew Mandy down into his lap, settling her against his shoulder, holding her hand and toying with the engagement ring on her finger.

His brother shot him a knowing grin, and Caleb smiled back, marveling at how the years had melted away. On the airplane and later in the car, he and Reed had talked. They'd talked about their years as children and teenagers, what had happened to each of them after Caleb had left for Chicago and Reed's plans for the future.

Seth retrieved six champagne glasses from the china cabinet, setting them out on the dining-room table. "So, Caleb. Are you moving back here, or are you taking our sister away?"

"Both," said Caleb, casting a long glance at Mandy's profile. "We'll have to play it by ear to start. I'm hoping Reed won't mind if we stay at his place while we're in the valley."

"Welcome anytime," said Reed.

"Seriously?" Mandy asked in obvious surprise. "You're going to stay at your ranch?"

"Seriously," Caleb told her. "A very wise woman once told me I needed to change my perception of it."

He leaned in close to her ear. "I figure we'll need to make love in every room in the house."

She whispered back. "Not when Reed's around."

"What are you two whispering about?" asked Abigail as she appeared with a bottle of champagne.

"I'm sure you don't want to know," Travis sang, lifting the bottle from his sister's hands and peeling off the foil.

"I've been thinking," Caleb said to Reed, framing up an idea in his mind. "It's not really fair for Mandy and I to set up a permanent place in your house."

Reed frowned at him. "Why not?"

"I think we should be partners."

His brother shrugged. "Keep half of it if you want. But you're on the hook for the years we have a loss."

Caleb shook his head. "The ranch is yours. Danielle's already drafted up the papers. But I'll buy half of it back from you."

Reed scoffed out a laugh. "Right."

The champagne cork popped, and Abby laughed as the foam poured over Travis's hand.

"It's been recently appraised," Caleb noted. "So there'll be no trouble establishing a price."

Reed stared levelly across at him. "You think you're going to give me fifteen million dollars?"

"Fourteen five, actually. I hear the water rights are screwing with land values."

Abigail and Travis began handing around the full glasses.

"I'd take the offer," Seth told Reed.

"Don't be ridiculous," Reed countered.

"I'd play hardball if I was you," said Abigail. "Where's he going to find another ranch with such terrific neighbors?"

"Play hardball," Mandy agreed with her sister. She bopped the side of her head against Caleb's chest. "Give him the fifteen."

Then she sat up straighter and accepted a glass of champagne from her sister.

Travis handed one to Reed.

Reed brandished his own glass like a weapon. "I'm not taking any money for the ranch. And that's final."

"Mandy," Caleb intoned.

"Yes?" she answered, twisting her head to look at him.

"Please meddle."

She grinned, leaned in and gave him a very satisfying kiss on the lips. "Whatever you say, darling."

Caleb crooked his head to one side to paste Reed with a challenging look. "She's my secret weapon."

Seth raised his glass. "Congratulations, Caleb. You are the luckiest man in the world."

"Agreed," Caleb breathed.

Reed spoke up. "To the Jacobs and the Terrells. A new family."

"Here, here," everyone agreed, clinking glasses all around, then taking a drink.

"To my beautiful bride," Caleb whispered, gently touching his glass to Mandy's.

Her green eyes glowed with obvious joy. "Do you really want me to convince Reed to take the money?"

"Absolutely. Go get him, tiger."

* * * * *

PASSION

For a spicier, decidedly hotter read—
this is your destination for romance!

COMING NEXT MONTH
AVAILABLE FEBRUARY 14, 2012

#2137 TO KISS A KING
Kings of California
Maureen Child

#2138 WHAT HAPPENS IN CHARLESTON...
Dynasties: The Kincaids
Rachel Bailey

#2139 MORE THAN PERFECT
Billionaires and Babies
Day Leclaire

#2140 A COWBOY IN MANHATTAN
Colorado Cattle Barons
Barbara Dunlop

#2141 THE WAYWARD SON
The Master Vintners
Yvonne Lindsay

#2142 BED OF LIES
Paula Roe

You can find more information on upcoming Harlequin® titles,
free excerpts and more at www.HarlequinInsideRomance.com.

HDCNM0112

REQUEST YOUR FREE BOOKS!
2 FREE NOVELS PLUS 2 FREE GIFTS!

Harlequin®

Desire

ALWAYS POWERFUL, PASSIONATE AND PROVOCATIVE

YES! Please send me 2 FREE Harlequin Desire® novels and my 2 FREE gifts (gifts are worth about $10). After receiving them, if I don't wish to receive any more books, I can return the shipping statement marked "cancel." If I don't cancel, I will receive 6 brand-new novels every month and be billed just $4.30 per book in the U.S. or $4.99 per book in Canada. That's a saving of at least 14% off the cover price! It's quite a bargain! Shipping and handling is just 50¢ per book in the U.S. and 75¢ per book in Canada.* I understand that accepting the 2 free books and gifts places me under no obligation to buy anything. I can always return a shipment and cancel at any time. Even if I never buy another book, the two free books and gifts are mine to keep forever.

225/326 HDN FEF3

Name	(PLEASE PRINT)	
Address		Apt. #
City	State/Prov.	Zip/Postal Code

Signature (if under 18, a parent or guardian must sign)

Mail to the **Reader Service:**
IN U.S.A.: P.O. Box 1867, Buffalo, NY 14240-1867
IN CANADA: P.O. Box 609, Fort Erie, Ontario L2A 5X3

Not valid for current subscribers to Harlequin Desire books.

Want to try two free books from another line?
Call 1-800-873-8635 or visit www.ReaderService.com.

* Terms and prices subject to change without notice. Prices do not include applicable taxes. Sales tax applicable in N.Y. Canadian residents will be charged applicable taxes. Offer not valid in Quebec. This offer is limited to one order per household. All orders subject to credit approval. Credit or debit balances in a customer's account(s) may be offset by any other outstanding balance owed by or to the customer. Please allow 4 to 6 weeks for delivery. Offer available while quantities last.

Your Privacy—The Reader Service is committed to protecting your privacy. Our Privacy Policy is available online at www.ReaderService.com or upon request from the Reader Service.

We make a portion of our mailing list available to reputable third parties that offer products we believe may interest you. If you prefer that we not exchange your name with third parties, or if you wish to clarify or modify your communication preferences, please visit us at www.ReaderService.com/consumerschoice or write to us at Reader Service Preference Service, P.O. Box 9062, Buffalo, NY 14269. Include your complete name and address.

HDES11B

Rhonda Nelson

SIZZLES WITH ANOTHER INSTALLMENT OF

When former ranger Jack Martin is assigned to
provide security to Mariette Levine, a local pastry
chef, he believes this will be an open-and-shut case.
Yet the danger becomes all too real when Mariette is
attacked. But things aren't always what they seem,
and soon Jack's protective instincts demand he save
the woman he is quickly falling for.

THE KEEPER

**Available February 2012
wherever books are sold.**

Louisa Morgan loves being around children.
So when she has the opportunity to tutor bedridden Ellie,
she's determined to bring joy back into the motherless
girl's world. Can she also help Ellie's father open his
heart again? Read on for a sneak peek of

THE COWBOY FATHER

by Linda Ford,
available February 2012 from Love Inspired Historical.

Why had Louisa thought she could do this job? A bubble of self-pity whispered she was totally useless, but Louisa ignored it. She wasn't useless. She could help Ellie if the child allowed it.

Emmet walked her out, waiting until they were out of earshot to speak. "I sense you and Ellie are not getting along."

"Ellie has lost her freedom. On top of that, everything is new. Familiar things are gone. Her only defense is to exert what little independence she has left. I believe she will soon tire of it and find there are more enjoyable ways to pass the time."

He looked doubtful. Louisa feared he would tell her not to return. But after several seconds' consideration, he sighed heavily. "You're right about one thing. She's lost everything. She can hardly be blamed for feeling out of sorts."

"She hasn't lost everything, though." Her words were quiet, coming from a place full of certainty that Emmet was more than enough for this child. "She has you."

"She'll always have me. As long as I live." He clenched his fists. "And I fully intend to raise her in such a way that even if something happened to me, she would never feel like I was gone. I'd be in her thoughts and in her actions every day."

Peace filled Louisa. "Exactly what my father did."

Their gazes connected, forged a single thought about fathers and daughters...how each needed the other. How sweet the relationship was.

Louisa tipped her head away first. "I'll see you tomorrow."

Emmet nodded. "Until tomorrow then."

She climbed behind the wheel of their automobile and turned toward home. She admired Emmet's devotion to his child. It reminded her of the love her own father had lavished on Louisa and her sisters. Louisa smiled as fond memories of her father filled her thoughts. Ellie was a fortunate child to know such love.

Louisa understands what both father and daughter are going through. Will her compassion help them heal—and form a new family? Find out in
THE COWBOY FATHER
by Linda Ford, available February 14, 2012.

Love Inspired Books celebrates 15 years of inspirational romance in 2012! February puts the spotlight on Love Inspired Historical, with each book celebrating family and the special place it has in our hearts. Be sure to pick up all four Love Inspired Historical stories, available February 14, wherever books are sold.

USA TODAY bestselling author

Sarah Morgan

brings readers another enchanting story

ONCE A FERRARA WIFE...

When Laurel Ferrara is summoned back to Sicily
by her estranged husband, billionaire
Cristiano Ferrara, Laurel knows things are about
to heat up. And Cristiano's power is a potent
reminder of his Sicilian dynasty's unbreakable rule:
once a Ferrara wife, always a Ferrara wife....

Sparks fly this February

HP13049